GAME DAY

A KODIAKS WEDDING NOVELLA

KING OF THE COURT
BOOK FOUR

PIPER LAWSON

Line and copy editing by Cassie Robertson
Proofreading by Devon Burke
Cover design by Emily Wittig

GAME DAY

A KING OF THE COURT WEDDING NOVELLA

In the heat of victory, I asked her to be mine forever.

We'd both triumphed in our own way:

Nova broke free from her past.

I led my team to a championship and discovered life beyond the court.

Our journey to "I do" was supposed to be easy.

Except...

The hottest resort in Aspen is only available on short notice.

A new season with the Denver Kodiaks looms on the horizon.

My parents are too obsessed with my career to get to know the woman who stole my heart.

Add dueling bridesmaids, last-minute chaos, and a life-changing decision.

With love and loyalty on the line, it's time to score the most important win of our lives.

GAME DAY is a King of the Court wedding novella and should be read following Play Maker (King of the Court #3).

Get ready for fun and games with Clay, Nova and all your favorite Kodiaks!

For anyone who's decided
"my forever starts
today"

NOVA

"*MARRY ME, CLAY!*" The woman next to me in the arrivals lounge screams it loudly enough my ears ring.

For a girl who grew up in a trailer clutching a sketchpad, I love a crowd. Being part of a bigger whole—one where every person shares a common dream, breathes the same air is exhilarating.

That was what I expected when I drove here today: a few loyal, bleary-eyed fans camped out to receive the Denver Kodiaks basketball team at their early-morning arrival.

Instead, I'm wedged elbow to elbow with hundreds of crazed Kodashians clutching

Starbucks and phones and posters at the airport.

This is less *Ted Lasso* and more *Hunger Games.*

I swallow a giggle. I'm going to laugh about this.

If I survive.

The glass doors from the arrivals area slide open with a whoosh, and the crowd waiting on this side bumps into one another like excited ping-pong balls.

"It's not them," the screamer's friend says, nodding toward the cluster of tall guys in suits emerging.

Disappointment crashes over the lounge in a wave, manic faces falling with dejection.

The woman who had screamed her proposal lowers her matching sign.

The men are big, but they're not who everyone is here for.

The legends.

The champs.

It was supposed to be private knowledge when the team's plane, which was delayed due to a storm, was landing after their preseason road trip, but every fan in town—

possibly every adult in Colorado—is here to greet them.

I'm adjusting my plain, white ball cap, my pink hair tucked up under it, when my phone buzzes in my pocket.

Brooke: You regretting this idea yet?

I lift my phone, elbows pressed to my sides by the crowd, and type back.

Nova: Ask me again if I get trampled in the next hour.

A yipping at my feet is followed by a French bulldog weaving between my legs until I'm tangled in his leash.

"Waffles! Don't make me regret bringing you," I murmur, adjusting my feet on either side of his body to protect him—and so I can scoop him up at a moment's notice if things get messy.

His noises lower to a whimper, but he's still vibrating with excitement.

I know how he feels. I wanted to come today not only to bring the Frenchie, whom

I've been dog-sitting for the week because his regular sitter was sick, back to Miles, but to greet Clay when he sets foot back in Denver.

Clayton Wade.

All star.

MVP.

As of three weeks ago, my fiancé.

The man who taught me to believe in myself no matter what.

I've loved him since the moment I laid eyes on his huge, stoic gorgeousness, and if he's telling the truth, he fell pretty damn fast himself.

I miss the hell out of him. A few days without his growly presence, and I'm starting to feel like the grumpy one.

Brooke: If those Kodashians come at you, I'll come for them.

Nova: Don't go down for murder on my account.

Brooke: Justifiable homicide. That's what friends are for.

A shriek splits the arrivals lounge.

"They're here!!! For real!" The first woman bounces on her toes.

More tall men emerge from the arrivals doors, and I don't need to recognize their faces to know it's them.

The crowd surges toward the Kodiaks team, security overwhelmed trying to hold them off.

The "Marry Me, Clay!" sign was abandoned the moment the first woman caught sight of her dream guy.

Another woman is saying, "Oh my God," over and over.

Still another is stripping off her shirt.

Oh boy.

I will not die in a pile of high-heeled boots and clutch bags.

Self-preservation kicks in. I grab Waffles and hug him to me as we're pushed toward the doors with the wave.

I catch glimpses over the crowd.

Atlas first. The tallest of the guys, with his buzzed head and Beats headphones.

Then Miles, his trademark cocky grin flashing as he says something over his shoulder to Jay, who's laughing reluctantly.

Then I see him.

He's wearing a backward hat and gray hoodie, the black LV bag I picked out for him to match mine draped over one shoulder. My breath sticks in my chest. Not only because there's barely enough room to breathe, but because his presence and intensity sucks the oxygen from the entire arrivals lounge.

The grumpy player I met and fell for on an airplane two years ago.

I had a panic attack on my way to my sister's wedding, and he saved me.

I'd thought we'd never see each other again, but it turned out he was on my brother-in-law's team.

We had to keep it a secret, but every second was thrilling. Sexy. Unbelievable.

Kind of like Clay himself.

He scans the crowd, searching for something.

Or someone.

"Clay!" I shout, but a hundred other fans are doing exactly the same.

I take a step backward, not for my own sake, but because Waffles has tiny bones and I'll never forgive myself if he gets hurt.

Clay doesn't hear me. He frowns and continues on his way.

"Dammit," I curse. I wanted to be the first to tell him welcome home.

Mission failed, I start to type to Brooke.

Right when I'm trying to catch my breath, the crowd parts.

Then he's there.

Six feet, five inches of male, honed for destruction on the basketball court. Black tattoos emerge from under his sleeves, twining around his wrists as if even the ink can't get enough.

His eyes lock on mine, and he stalks toward me, ignoring the meltdown of fans and clicking camera phones.

The fans scream louder, hands fumbling for phones and angling for the perfect selfie.

Clay's easy strides eat up the distance between us. Security's hot on his heels, but Clay doesn't care.

A woman starts crying next to me, her hand over her mouth like she's close to touching Mother Teresa.

If Mother Teresa had muscles for days and averaged twenty-five a game in the finals.

He stops in front of me, and it's as if all the oxygen is sucked from the arrivals lounge.

My heart hammers as if we've never been this close before. As if I've been waiting my entire life for him to look at me like I'm the home he's desperate for.

"You came." His eyes crinkle at the corners.

"Surprise. I wanted to bring tequila but ran out of hands," I say.

Clay reaches for my hat and tugs it off, letting my pink hair tumble down around my shoulders.

"Got all I need right here."

He drags me up on my toes. His hard lips crush down on mine, and every thought in my mind evaporates at the feel of him.

He kisses me like he's been counting the days, the hours, the minutes until I'm back in his arms.

The season might be barreling down on us, but none of it matters in this moment. I never feel as alive, as real, as vibrant as when I'm in his arms. As if I'm the prize he's worked every day for.

Waffles squirms in my arms, and I reluctantly pull back.

Clay leans closer, lips brushing my ear. "You tell anyone our plan?"

I shake my head, a shiver going through me. "Not a soul."

He drops his lips to my forehead and threads his fingers in mine.

The "Marry Me, Clay!" sign disappears under my feet as we head for the doors together.

NOVA

"Dammit. The boutique owner I was supposed to meet had an emergency." Brooke taps her nails on the hood of the car and frowns at her phone.

I scan the parking lot tucked between beautiful brick buildings. "We can wait for her?"

"No. I'll reschedule. We can talk about her designs another time."

I stifle my yawn, trying to let the brisk air and mountain views invigorate me. I promised to ride shotgun with Brooke on a day trip to Aspen without knowing I'd be doing it on three hours of sleep.

"I get it," Brooke teases as she tucks the

phone away. "I'm not as riveting as a certain basketball player who came back into town in the early hours of this morning."

By the time I got Waffles back to Miles and Clay and I arrived home, it was eight. Clay was beat. A feeling I can completely understand now.

"You're every bit as riveting," I promise. "Besides, who needs sleep when you have friends?"

Brooke loops her arm in mine, and we head toward Galena Street.

I get why tourists flock here by the thousands. It's not their peak season of snow flurries and après-ski drinks, but the trees and changing colors and the mountains provide a breathtaking background for cozy cafés, fabulous stores and chalet-style hotels.

"How is engaged life?" Brooke asks, the gravel crunching under our boots.

"Well. The media interest in Clay seems to have dialed up more, which I didn't think was possible."

"The only thing better than a championship is a championship followed by the MVP getting married," she says with a nod.

"Speaking of, Jay told me the team is invited to the mayor's house for dinner tonight."

"Apparently, she's a big fan of basketball, or has been since they won in June."

"Everyone wants a piece of them."

"I hope there's a piece of him left for me," I joke, but there's some truth to it.

"There are a lot of road trips ahead. I wouldn't toss your vibrator in the trash yet." My friend points at a boutique, and we head for it.

As we cross the street, I'm thinking about the schedule bearing down on us. Now that the Kodiaks have won the championship, it's not only the regular games and workouts but a whole additional slate of appearances, contracts, and promotions.

All of which is an honor most people would kill for, I remind myself.

I resolve to be happy about it as I hold the door for her, and little bells tinkle over the doorway as we step inside.

"Oh, these are gorgeous." I'm drawn immediately to a rack displaying cozy sweaters, and Brooke heads past me for another with leggings. I turn over a price tag and swallow.

Brooke peeks over my shoulder. "You should buy one in each color."

Part of me will probably never get accustomed to the reality that I can afford the things I need—plus the ones I want and pretty much anything I decide I like.

I reach for a sexy black dress, and Brooke hums her approval.

"Yes, you need to try that on. You could wear it to the mayor's house. In case Clay needs a reminder to be more interested in scoring *off* the court."

I laugh as she grabs two pairs of leggings and a skirt off the rack and nudges me toward the changing rooms.

"So," she starts from inside the next changing room. "With the craziness of the season approaching, have you started wedding planning?"

Her sly voice has me smiling. I can't get anything past my friend.

A tingle of excitement runs through me as I work off my jeans and tug my sweater over my head.

We have talked about it.

The weekend after Clay proposed, when I

was trying to find my things in the second bedroom of his condo.

"Have you seen my winter clothes? I swear I have some I haven't used since before LA."

"We need a bigger house," he grunted as he found me rifling through boxes in the closet.

"It's fine," I insisted.

The summer was so busy with the Kodiaks winning and my art taking off that we hadn't had time to get anything else.

He helped me up and brought me out to the patio to drink a bottle of wine.

"Is it weird that every time I look at flowers, I think about marrying you?" I asked.

His lips lifted. "I like that everything reminds you of marrying me. I don't want to wait a year to do it."

The conviction in his voice made my heart skip.

"If we do it during the season, no one can come," I pointed out. "The only break is all-star week." Which would be hardly any time off for Clay and his friends.

"It's not for them, Pink," he said as he brushed his lips over mine. "Only person I need there is you."

Seriously. Is this man even real?

That was when I had a crazy idea.

I blurted it out on the heels of cabernet and dreaming on our patio.

At first, Clay cocked his head, brows lifting.

But the more we talked about it, the more we liked it.

Now, Brooke's waiting for me to respond.

"At first we were thinking of getting married after next season," I start. "That way, everyone from the league would be available."

"But the talk will be about the team," she says immediately. "If they ran it back, if they came up short."

"Exactly." I finish pulling on the dress and step outside as Brooke sweeps her curtain wide as well.

The leggings make her toned legs look even better. "Your ass it amazing in those," I say with a little envy.

"Hello sexy pot, I'm kettle," she says with an eyeroll. "You need to buy that dress."

I turn in the mirror, enjoying how the fabric clings to my curves. With my pink hair, it's edgy and chic. "Fine. You're a dangerous wingwoman."

"You mean the best," she corrects. "But for real. What are you planning?"

Brooke is one of my closest friends, and I can't keep the secret from her.

"We're going to elope."

She gasps, a hand flying to her mouth. "No fucking way!"

Her entire demeanor changes from excited to horrified in an instant.

I'm still processing her reaction when another curtain sweeps wide behind me and a familiar voice says, "Did I hear someone's getting married?!"

I swivel so fast I nearly trip.

The redhead wearing the same black dress is taller than me, with endlessly long legs and bangs and long, wavy Dakota Johnson hair. As effortlessly cool as she looks, her smile is warm and her golden eyes glint with mischief.

"Annie! What are you doing here?" I rush to my West Coast friend and throw my arms around her.

I introduce her and Brooke and they exchange a warm greeting.

"Rae's DJing here in a few weeks, and we came to scope out the place. I'm meeting her for lunch at Little Nell. You ladies have to come," Annie insists.

Brooke and I exchange a look. I can tell she's dying to talk about the wedding, but this is too good to pass up.

Ten minutes later, we're getting out of the car at Little Nell.

"What is this place?" I ask.

"Only the most incredible resort in all of Aspen." Brooke claps her palms for emphasis.

As if to back her up, the scenery opens up to reveal a gorgeous vista of pine trees and mountains, the main lodge rising majestically from the center.

We head inside with Annie. Surrounding us are high ceilings and wooden beams. It's like a holiday card.

"This is amazing," I murmur.

"Why are you whispering?" Annie laughs.

"It feels like a library. Or a temple. Or both."

We wind through to the dining room,

where we meet Rae. We take our seats and order drinks and food.

"Okay ladies, we have a serious topic." Brooke clasps her hands and looks solemnly between us as she lowers her voice. "Our mutual friend and her hulking hunk are planning to elope."

Evidently, she couldn't wait until later to talk about it.

"Well?!" she prompts when neither Annie nor Rae responds immediately. "Tell her it's a terrible idea. That she'll miss out on the wedding planning and the guests and the cake and the party. Flowers everywhere and too much champagne and people telling bad stories about her."

Rae lifts a shoulder. "She should do what she wants."

"I was totally going to buy your next album, but now..." Brooke sends a pointed look at Annie.

"Tyler and I got married on an island with a short guest list," she starts, referring to her next-level–famous rock star husband. "Partly, we did it because we were afraid of it being made public. We found out the hard way that you can only control so much." Her lips twist wryly.

"You regret it?" I ask, curious.

"Not a second. Are you eloping because you really want to? Or you're worried it will be too out of control if you do it here?"

Three pairs of eyes turn to me as I consider.

I would marry Clay anytime, anywhere and it would be a dream come true. But, I'd be lying if I said the circus around him didn't affect our plans.

"Maybe a little bit of both," I admit.

I steer the conversation to Rae's upcoming performances, trying to escape being in the hot seat.

"This isn't even the best part of the resort," Brooke weighs in as we rise after the meal. "Is the deck open?" she asks the hostess at the front of the restaurant.

Her smile is sympathetic. "It's booked for an event this evening."

"We'll be quick and leave zero trace," Brooke offers. "Promise."

The hostess reluctantly shows us out the back to a huge sweeping field with a panoramic mountain view.

My breath lodges in my throat. "Oh, wow."

It's staggeringly beautiful. The bright blue sky, the craggy peaks.

Nature is showing off. It's a spectacle, the grandiosity of the landscape and the resort tucked into the heart of it. A way for us mere humans to experience the world the way it was meant to be.

Brooke sets up to take a selfie, and I grin.

"I came for photos," she insists. "I'm not leaving without one."

The four of us lean in. "Now pretend you're not famous," Brooke instructs after we take a cute smiling pic. "This one's for friends only. Or blackmail. Because is someone really a friend if you don't have blackmail material on them?"

We laugh and make faces at the camera.

It's refreshing to be around women whose company I enjoy, ones who have no expectations beyond friendship and mutual support and respect. I didn't realize I've missed this lately.

As Brooke posts the more presentable photo to social, my mind drifts back to our wedding conversation.

When Clay and I talked about running away together, we focused on all the benefits. Ease. Speed. Privacy. We didn't talk much about what we'd be giving up.

Maybe there are more downsides to eloping than we fully acknowledged.

I take another second to admire the scenery when my phone rings.

Call from Clay.

"Hey," I answer.

"Hi, Pink."

My heart lifts when I hear his voice.

"How big a room do you need for painting?" he asks.

"I have my studio in town."

"Yeah, but if our place was bigger."

Suspicion rises up. "Where are you?"

"Ah. Nowhere. Where are you?"

I want to ask him again what he's doing and why he's being weird about it, but the girls are here, so I say, "Little Nell in Aspen. It feels like we're in the very heart of nature."

"Only with five-star dining," Annie calls.

"And shopping," Brooke weighs in.

"Imagine exchanging vows in this place." I text him photos of the sweeping views. "Just you and the mountains and the person you want to spend the rest of your life with. It's incredibly romantic."

"Romantic, huh?" The smile in his tone makes me smile, too.

Distant voices come over the line, the words inaudible.

"I should go," Clay says, but it's grudging. "Meet you back at the condo before the mayor's dinner."

"Sure. And Clay."

"Yeah, Pink?"

I bite my lip. "Can I drive?"

3

NOVA

"You're trying to kill me."

Clay's low drawl skims along my skin as he adjusts his legs in the passenger seat.

I give him a once over from the driver's seat of the BMW I bought this summer. "I drive perfectly well."

"I meant the dress."

The black cocktail dress was a good move. I love the tiny straps and the way the fabric skims my body, dipping between my breasts and ending partway down my thighs. My hair is down in waves that swoop across my collarbones, ending at my shoulders.

"Oh, this?" I shift in my seat, exposing more thigh. "I bought it today. I'm glad you like it."

Clay makes a sound between a grunt and an exhale as if the extra skin I'm showing is physically hurting him.

A tux always looks good on a man. A custom tux on a man like Clay is the biggest turn-on imaginable.

His dark ink snakes out from the cuffs and his shirt collar, the expensive fabric pulling across the expanse of muscle he works on every day.

It's enough of a distraction that I barely notice the feel of the beautiful sports car, which is the whole reason I wanted to drive.

"So, you and Brooke had fun in Aspen," my fiancé says, bringing me back.

"Little Nell was amazing." My lips curve as I picture the dreamy landscape.

"Amazing enough you're questioning Paris?" he asks after a moment.

"No," I say quickly. "We agreed to elope. It's simpler that way. Our schedule's crazy and this way, we can do it on our own time."

"My schedule's crazy," he corrects, regret lacing his voice.

"It's ours now." I toss him a smile. "Besides, Little Nell is booked up for ages."

"Ahh." He's teasing. "They'd make room for us. I'm kind of a big deal around here, Pink."

"So I keep hearing." I laugh. "But it was beautiful. For a moment I could see it."

"You're beautiful. Especially when you smile."

I flush with pleasure. I never get over this man's compliments.

"We have to get to dinner." It's a question he's asking, though it sounds like a statement.

"It's at the mayor's house. And it's for you," I remind him. "You have a better plan?"

The mayor invited the entire team, including some of the management. I'm not sure who else is on the guest list, but can only assume there will also be a number of city brass.

"Yeah. You could pull over and let me do the things I've been thinking about all week," he drawls.

My breath catches.

Maybe I should have expected it, but after a few days of coffee dates with Brooke, then a visit with Mari and Emily, all I wanted was to hear his voice. To wake up next to him, his strong, tattooed arms pulling me close in bed.

Focus.

"It has been a long week," I admit.

"For me too. Figured after I put a ring on your finger, I'd sleep easier. Guess I was wrong about that."

Warmth tingles along the exposed skin of my thigh.

Clay's hand.

Before I met him, I never thought much about the importance of chemistry in a relationship. Since then, I can't stop the flare of desire that sneaks up at the most inopportune moments.

He's drawing circles, or letters, imprinting each one on my flesh like a tattoo I'd give every dollar I have to read.

"What's under the dress?" he asks.

My eyelids threaten to drift closed. I squint at the road in front of me.

"Practically nothing."

"If you mean that, we're not making it anywhere near the mayor's house."

He's so sexy. The way he says it, matter-of-fact, makes me want to forget dinner, too.

"Play nice with the mayor and you can have me however you want."

"Deal."

I'm caught off guard by his quick agreement.

At least until he adds, "Now show me."

In the rearview mirror, my eyes are fringed with dark, mascara-covered lashes. My lips are coated with matte pink lipstick. The flush on my cheeks is all him.

There's barely any traffic on the road.

I reach under my dress and tug it up. Switching my hands on the wheel, I go to the other side and work that up to reveal the pink lace thong.

Clay's hand flexes on my thigh.

"When we're married, half of what's mine is yours."

"I suppose." I'm not sure where he's going with this.

"Which also means half of what's yours is mine."

"And my Sanrio T-shirt collection will be worth millions one day," I deadpan. "Did you have something in mind?"

"Those." He nods to my panties. "Take them off."

I bite my lip. The blood pounding in my veins says I can, I even want to.

I work my panties down over my hips and one leg. Then to the other, switching feet carefully to take them off.

"Happy?" I toss them at Clay.

He catches them, tucking them in his pocket. "Not nearly."

We're driving down the road in the dark, on our way to a dinner with dignitaries and tuxes.

Drake throbs from the radio. Clay's hand returns to my thigh, tracing slow shapes that inch higher and higher.

"There's a mansion full of people waiting to tell you how incredible you are," I whisper.

Clay shifts closer. "I'd rather hear it from you."

Arousal chases through me, his touch like fire blazing along my skin and twisting low in my stomach.

At a red light, I turn toward him and see him watching me. He's statue-still except for the tic in his jaw.

I shift in the seat, but when his touch strokes up the inside of my thigh, my knees fall open.

His fingers move higher, skimming across my skin to where I'm already aching.

"We don't have time to stop," I manage.

"Then you better keep those pretty eyes on the road."

When he brushes between my legs where I'm throbbing, I could cry.

"So fucking soft," he groans. "Love how you feel bare."

He strokes me, rubbing light, insistent circles like he'd traced in my leg...

Only now they're far more intimate.

I gasp with pleasure as he plays with my clit, lighting up every aching part of me.

His fingers press inside me. I tilt up my hips because, God help me, there's nothing I want more than the way he makes me feel.

"Tell me you haven't been this wet all week," he murmurs.

"I have two perfectly good hands and a vibrator." It's my best attempt at trash talk, and he sees through it.

"They're the bench, Pink. I'm the starting lineup."

Clay does his best work on a basketball court. His second-best work is between my thighs.

I sneak a look down to see his tattooed arm disappearing under my dress. His muscles flex in a way that's beyond sexy.

The GPS interrupts us with instructions to turn.

We're five minutes from the mayor's house. There's no time for what he's doing, but I can't find the willpower or the words to stop him.

His finger wedges between the seat and my body, pressing up inside me. He's thick and determined.

I catch a glimpse of my eyes in the rearview mirror. Pupils blown, cheeks flushed.

He slips past my defenses, finds my weak spots, makes me beg. The tension builds in me, overwhelming.

Clay groans. "You have no idea how hard it was on the road without you."

It's going to get harder, I think but don't say it.

This is what he signed up for. What *I* signed up for by loving him.

"We'll be late," I whisper.

"They'll wait. I'm not going anywhere until my future wife comes all over these fingers."

Clay presses a second finger inside me, stretching my body even as it feels like my chest is ripping in two.

He's not only touching me, he's staking his claim. There's something territorial about the way he handles me. He's as at home with my body as he is on the court, spinning a special kind of magic that sprouts inside me and hums to the rhythm of his fingers.

My other hand is pressed against the steering wheel, my diamond ring glinting stubbornly in the near darkness.

My hips snap toward him, the leather seat smooth against my skin.

"That's it. Come for me, sweetheart," he groans.

Pleasure rockets through me. My voice bounces off the interior of the BMW.

I ride out the feeling, chasing every ounce of pleasure as if I need it to live.

He pistons his fingers, demanding more of

my response until I'm trembling, my body wracked with aftershocks.

"How do you get more beautiful every day?" Clay murmurs as he withdraws. It's unhurried, like everything with him.

"How do your hands get bigger every day?" I counter, brushing a damp piece of hair out of my face as I feel the twinge of emptiness now that he's gone.

His smug grin flashes in the dark. "You know that's just the warm up."

Like this, with him, I can forget the world outside. There's no season starting in two weeks. There's only us in this moment.

At least until the mayor's house looms a few hundred feet away.

The gates are open, the gravel driveway curving up in front of a huge mansion. I pull up behind a Mercedes and put the car in park before checking my appearance.

Clay pulls something out of his breast pocket—*my panties*—wipes his fingers on them and tucks them away again.

I'm still buzzing as I reach for the door handle. I toss the keys to the valet and take Clay's arm to head up the stairs.

"Looking wobbly in those shoes, Pink."

The warmth in his voice shoots down my spine, playing like his fingers where I can still feel them.

"And here I used to wish you'd talk more."

His chuckle echoes in the night.

4

CLAY

On my list of things I want to spend an evening off doing, having dinner at a politician's house is right up there with a root canal.

However, tonight is a celebration of the team and the city, so it's part of the gig.

Plus, I promised my girl I'd be on my best behavior.

The table's big enough to hold thirty. Nova and I are seated near the mayor and her husband. Jay's on Nova's other side, plus Chloe next to him. My gaze flicks between them, and Chloe registers first.

"I'm here representing Harlan. Jay and I are not together," she explains.

"Yeah, because you would never," Jay says, leaning over the table.

I swallow a chuckle.

It might have been years since they dated, but he's still one who gets under her skin.

Don't I know how it is.

I glance Nova's way because it's too fucking hard not to when she's near. Either I'm weak from days on the road, or she got prettier while I was gone. She looked sexy as hell when she put on that dress, and it was all I could do not to drag her into the backseat and remind us both why she's it for me.

My first few years in the league, I'd get off the plane after a trip and give anything for a burger, an ice bath, and my bed, not necessarily in that order. But now when I land on solid ground, I crave her.

My girl.

My fiancée.

Soon to be my wife.

My life has gotten better over the past year, and it's not only winning a championship with the guys I care about. It's her. Nova's the best part of my day, one I got used to with the downtime in the off-season.

At a promotional event this summer, I caught up with another all-star who confided that his wife was leaving him. Said he realized too late that he didn't pay enough attention to his wife.

I vow never to take mine for granted.

That's why in the moments between practices and team meetings for the past few months, I've been working on a little project.

It's taking more time than I thought, and keeping it a secret is getting harder.

My condo isn't nearly enough for the two of us, plus when I'm away for games, Nova deserves a roof that's hers.

I'm on a mission to find her the perfect house.

I've made her a silent promise that I'll have it before we walk down the aisle. When she swears to love me forever, I want her to know how committed I already am.

Today when I called her to ask about studio space from a house my realtor was showing me, I almost let it slip.

I blame it on the traveling and lack of sleep. I'll do better.

Waitstaff serve the first course, and before we finish our salads, the lights are dimming as the mayor rises from her seat.

"Thank you all for coming. Tonight, we're gathered here to honor our own," says the mayor. "I was elected last year and got to see the meteoric rise of this team. The Kodiaks have been a local fixture for years, but it's as if they came out of nowhere."

"If by 'out of nowhere,' you mean working our asses off for the last twenty years, then sure," Jay comments under his breath from beside Nova.

I resist the urge to snort.

"Now they're about to kick off another season, carrying the weight of an entire state on their shoulders."

Nova's hand is warm as it finds mine beneath the table.

I wish to hell we were alone right now. The feel of her in the car wasn't nearly enough.

I'm a methodical guy, and I've been thinking of all the things I'd do to her, with her, once I got back from our road trip, and—

"Clayton Wade."

I rise from my seat to applause, nodding grudgingly at everyone in the room.

"Would you please join me?" the mayor asks.

That's when I spot the flat, square box she's holding.

Evidently, there are gifts to go with dinner.

I like being the best, but it's enough to know I won. I don't need to stick around for pats on the back.

But she's waiting, and I have a feeling Nova wouldn't much like it if I hung the mayor out to dry in her own house.

I round the table and stand next to the woman, towering over her. She doesn't seem cowed in the slightest, one thing I like about her.

"This is for your tremendous contributions to the city of Denver." She lifts the lid to reveal an oversized gold key. "Both so far and in the future," she adds, though the crowd probably can't hear her over their applause. "Would you like to say a few words?"

I don't do speeches. In the locker room, they're necessary, but here it feels gratuitous.

But Nova's watching me, her eyes shining with pride and expectation.

I turn the key in my hands. It's sort of like a trophy, smooth and gold, and I've accepted my share of those.

"Thanks for this." I lift it in the air and nod to the room. "I'm sure it'll open a lot of doors."

The guys are cracking up before I reach my seat.

Miles turns the key in his hands. "Think this actually unlocks something?"

"Yeah, a big treasure chest full of loot."

"Really?"

"Mhmm. Latest espresso maker and everything," Rookie quips, and Miles snorts.

I've made the rounds, shaking hands and accepting congratulations from CEOs and a mix of public officials.

I'm talking with Miles and Rookie, Miles demanding to see my key up close.

Nova leans against my side, and I wrap an arm around her to tug her closer.

She stretches up on her toes to whisper, "I'm proud of you for making nice with all these people."

"I *can* play nice, you know."

"But it makes you so grumpy to do it." She's teasing, and I want to kiss the smile off her face.

I settle for stroking my knuckles down her bare arm. "Depends on the company."

"I mean it, though. You're a big deal here. You inspire so many fans to love the sport, to get involved, to feel proud of where they've grown roots, whether it's for a short time or forever."

I want to make a joke, but there's a seed of satisfaction in my chest.

I'm determined to make her proud, to be the man she thinks I am.

A throat clears at my elbow. The mayor and her husband are standing next to Nova and me.

"I hate to interrupt, but I do want to speak with the man of the hour," the mayor says with a wide smile.

The guys clear out, and Nova starts to as well, but I take her hand. *Stay*, I say without words.

"I need a fresh drink," she murmurs, then presses up onto her toes to whisper near my ear. "You've got this. There's no one in the entire league you can't take one on one."

"Thanks for the pep talk," I grumble as I watch her go.

"You two are really the most lovely couple. You met your girlfriend here in Denver?" the mayor asks.

"Fiancée," I correct.

Her eyes round. "There must be something magic in the water here."

A waiter offers me a drink from his tray. I ignore the champagne and grab a club soda instead.

"Listen, Clay," the mayor starts. "My secret agenda, if you can call it that, is that I'm hoping to secure your commitment as an ambassador of the city going forward into the new season."

The mayor wants visibility. A poster child.

I twist off the top of my club soda and down half the bottle.

"That's flattering, but I already have a job."

"Of course." She sips her wine. "But you're also a local hero for the Denver area at a time when so much attention will focus on the team.

When I mentioned this to James, he agreed completely."

I resist the temptation to swear. The team's owner would be only too happy to commit us to doing more, as long as it brings in more money, profile and opportunities to the club.

Nova catches my eye from the bar. The guys are keeping her company, making her smile and laugh.

I've got a few minutes left in me before I throw her over my shoulder and walk her out of here.

The thought of my fiancée, including the deal we made earlier and my promise to play nice, is the only thing that keeps me from telling the mayor exactly where she can shove her request.

"I'll do what I can," I hear myself say.

"Oh, that's wonderful. You won't regret it." The mayor's eyes brighten with triumph.

I excuse myself and cut across the room to my future wife.

Being here with these people, seeing how easily Nova fits in and makes friends, reminds me how everything in my life comes back to her.

I used to be about basketball, first, second, only.

Now, my heart doesn't beat without this angel with pink hair and a heart the size of a mountain whose smile lights up an entire room.

When I reach her side, she's already bouncing on her toes. "Well? What did the mayor want?"

"Help promoting the city."

"And you said..."

"I said I'd try my best."

Nova's eyes shine. "Good boy."

I swallow the groan as my hand finds her side. "You'll be a good girl later when you're coming on my cock," I murmur against her ear, loving the way she shivers.

But before I can drag her out of here, her phone buzzes from her purse. She glances at the screen, frowning. "Hello?" she answers.

A moment later, her gaze flies to mine.

"It's Little Nell," she whispers.

It takes a moment for my brain to catch up given all the blood in my body is fast-tracking it to my dick.

The resort she showed me looked like a slice of heaven, and the dreamy way she spoke about it earlier in the car made it clear it was *her* kind of heaven.

"Oh, really? Just a moment." She covers the handset. "They have a cancellation for the weekend before the home opener."

"You asked them to let you know if they had a spot," I deduce, amused.

"Maybe."

The expression on her face is eager and hopeful.

We talked about eloping, but now, it's obvious to at least one of us that she's got a new ambition.

When she looks like that, I want to give her anything. Everything.

"Tell me it's crazy," she whispers at me.

"It's crazy," I agree, but my tone makes it clear that crazy isn't a dealbreaker.

"We couldn't." Her eyes widen, and my lips twitch.

"We could."

Her brows shoot up. "Are you serious?"

"As a time-out with ten seconds left. If you still want to," I add.

Nova's excited inhale tells me everything I need to know. I stroke a thumb over her cheek.

"Then it's settled. I'll call Kat. You do Mari and Harlan."

"Okay. Let's do it." She beams.

We're getting married.

Right here in Colorado.

5

CLAY

"You too good to guard me, MVP?" Miles taunts.

He's dribbling up the court, and I'm matching his steps even though I'm going backward.

"You show me you did more than drink cappuccinos all summer, I'll get up on you," I respond.

"Drinking? No. Making? Yes. The six-week Barista Masters course I took was no joke. Did I tell you there was an—"

"Application to get accepted? Yeah, you mentioned it," Jay calls.

Miles lifts his jersey, and I don't need to look to see he's in as good shape as any of us.

It's a surprise that one of the most low-key guys I've ever played with decided to log the extra hours this summer, but a good one.

He breaks past me, squares up for a fadeaway, and sinks it.

Swish.

Slow clapping from the stands makes us look up. James is standing a few rows up, along with the mayor.

"Since when is this an open practice?" Jay asks under his breath.

"James and I were discussing how excited we are for the team's prospects for the coming season." The mayor's eyes run over us, landing on me as she smiles.

I'm not thrilled to see the suit who signs my paychecks standing with the woman who runs this city. Particularly the day her dinner party where I made some vague commitments, mostly out of devotion to my future bride.

The Kodiaks owner wasn't my favorite person even before he traded me to LA without my approval. We've made a fragile truce—I'm the most popular athlete in this city, and he doesn't want to piss off the fan base.

Still, this is another reminder of his tendency to overpromise.

On the court, my guys are organizing into formation for the next drill. Our capable coaching staff and trainers stand in huddles with clipboards and iPads. There's a spot in the rafters waiting for the banner we'll be unfurling at the first game of the season.

"Clay! Phone!" Rookie holds up the device from my seat.

Our coach shoots me a look. "No phones in practice."

"During the season," I correct.

He sighs as I jog across to get it.

I'm expecting a call from my realtor.

None of the two dozen houses he's has shown me over the past month have been right. Our budget is near limitless, but it's still hard to find a place with the other specs we want: close to the stadium for me. Close to Nova's sister and Harlan for her. A huge yard with room for gardens and picnics. A solarium she can transform into a studio to paint. Mountains in the distance because every time I see them, I think of us running through Red Rocks on our first date.

If we get married at Little Nell next weekend, my timeline to find the perfect home will shorten drastically.

But, it's not the realtor's number on my screen.

"Hey, sis," I answer as one of the trainers passes me a fresh Gatorade. I'm sweating more than I expected. Maybe I should've been working out with Miles this summer after all.

"What's so urgent I had to dodge my practicum to call you back?" Kat asks.

"I'm getting married next weekend." I keep my voice low. Announcing this in the middle of practice would derail today's drills more than any other interruption. "We were planning to elope, but Nova found a place here that she loves, and she wants to have a few friends and family there. We wanted to ask if you can make it."

She's quiet for so long I wonder if she hung up. "We'll be there. Of course, we will," comes a choked sound.

"Are you crying?!" I grunt.

Alarmed expressions flick to me from the guys, and I wave them off. *Kat,* I mouth.

"No!" She sniffs. "Daniel's not teaching and Andy will be out of school."

A feeling of satisfaction settles over me. "I'll send you more info after practice."

Coach is shooting me dagger-like glares, and I set the handset on the seat and hit speaker as I finish toweling off. I drop the fabric into a bin at the end of the row, narrowly missing one of our new rookies.

"Wait." Kat's syllable is sharp. "What about Mom and Dad?"

For a second, I'm not sure what she's asking. "I sent them an email a couple hours ago."

"You think they'll sit quietly in the back snapping photos and beaming?"

I shrug even though she can't see. "That's what everyone does at weddings."

Kat murmurs something that sounds like "God help us," but I'm already clicking off to avoid delaying practice further.

I toss the phone on my chair and jog back toward the court. When I get into position for the drill, everyone's watching me.

They can't have heard our conversation. But from their expressions, I'm wondering.

Miles crosses the court with a wide grin and sweaty arms wide. "What do you say. Are we invited?"

"I've been working on a speech for months." Jay clears his throat.

"Been wanting to wear these blue leather shoes," Rookie adds.

Miles hollers over the others. "You wouldn't be marrying Nova if it wasn't for me. I'm the one who brought you together in the first place."

So much for keeping it quiet until after practice.

I stare him down for a moment.

Two.

"Yeah, you're invited."

The guys jump on me.

6

NOVA

Five days until the wedding

"It's too much lace." Mari's nose wrinkles as her gaze rakes down the layers of cream thread and fabric.

"Is there such thing?" Brooke counters.

In the three days since we decided to move forward with this preseason wedding, Clay and I sat down with the wedding planner from the venue.

We went over numbers, ceremony plans, guest lists and scheduling.

Mari promptly came up with her own to-do list, which she insisted should be mine too.

As much as Clay said he wants to share the preparation, he's still pulled away for practice and I'm excited to have these moments with my sister and best friend.

Right now, they're holding up two sides of the same wedding gown.

"It's so... virginal," Mari insists.

Brooke blinks. "Then it's a good thing your sister is pure as the mountain powder."

Mari looks between us, eyes widening in disbelief as Brooke cracks up.

"Nova's obviously marrying Clay because he's such a poet."

Now we're both laughing, but my sister only shakes her head.

I insisted I didn't need a traditional wedding dress, but with a single phone call Brooke had one of the foremost wedding designers in Denver opening their doors to us on short notice.

So, I figured it would be uncharitable not to at least see what they have.

"A trumpet shape would make your hips

look…" Mari makes a swooping motion with her hands.

"But Nova has wanted a big puffy princess gown since she was a little girl," Brooke cuts in.

Mari scoffs. "How would you know that?"

Brooke turns to me. "I'll pull some more options. Don't move." She heads off to scope out some more gowns on the other side of the boutique.

Mari squares her shoulders and lowers her voice. "Listen, I know when you came for my wedding to Harlan, I picked Chloe over you as my maid of honor. And I've been meaning to tell you…" She lifts her shoulders. "That was a mistake. Not because Chloe's not amazing, but I know how capable you are."

My heart expands. "Thanks, Mar. I appreciate you being here, especially since Emily's not sleeping and you have that big project at work."

Her eyes shine, but she sniffs. "Yeah, well, you're my baby sister."

Brooke returns loaded down with dresses. "Here we go. Try these."

With the help of the store attendant, I try one dress after the other. Every cut and style.

"Hair up?" Mari suggests with one, and Brooke shakes her head.

As much as I love that they're both here, I wish they'd smile at the same time.

"What do *you* like?" the attendant asks me.

I look between the dresses and see one I haven't tried yet.

This gown is fitted across the top, with sheer panels and beaded ones in white and pale silver. The skirt flares out in cascading waves of taffeta.

It's definitely not subtle, but it is breathtaking.

The attendant helps me into it, the fabric hugging my curves in a way that makes me want to sigh.

Minutes later, I'm stepping onto the pedestal and meeting my eyes in the mirror.

My heart starts to hammer as I take in the woman before me. She's shimmery, elegant, and beaming.

I feel like a fairy princess.

I'm marrying the man of my dreams, so maybe it's right that my gown would be straight out of a fairytale.

"Whatever you're going to say," I caution, "I really like this one so..."

When I turn, Brooke's palm is pressed to her mouth and Mari's eyes are damp.

"Good," Mari responds, her lips curving.

Brooke nods with a little laugh. "It's beautiful."

My chest fills with anticipation and delight. I love the gown—since laying eyes on it, I can't stop imagining walking down the aisle in such a dreamy dress—but I'm thrilled they adore it too.

"We'd need to make a few alterations to the length," the attendant says. "When do you need it?"

"This weekend."

Mari intervenes, holding out a credit card. "Whatever it takes."

Brooke nods. "This wedding will be the best publicity you get all year."

Clay: Find a dress?

Nova: Maybe

Clay: Don't even think of paying for it

yourself. Whatever my wife wants, she gets.

My stomach does the little dance it always does when Clay says something sweet that also makes me want to climb him like a tree.

When I look up, Mari and Brooke are arguing over veils.

It feels good to be this loved.

I think.

I pay for the dress with Clay's black card, and the three of us head outside into the fall sunlight.

"We need to celebrate," Mari decides.

"With bubbly," Brooke jumps in.

"I want to be home for a delivery," I say. Clay's shoes are supposed to be arriving from Italy. "We have champagne there?"

The girls agree.

"Who else is coming?" Brooke asks.

I run her through the guest list, including with the team.

"We're going for intimate and informal," I

say. "No bridal parties, no special roles. This way everyone, including Kat and Clay's parents, can just show up and have a good time."

"I thought I was so ready to be married," Mari says from my shoulder.

"You were perfectly prepared. You had a checklist a mile long. And Chloe," I remind my sister.

"That's not what I mean. Being a wife is different from being a girlfriend. You're going to be dealing with his family, the public pressures..."

"All of which we've already dealt with," I insist.

On the way back to Clay's and my place, Brooke and I talk about the wedding and the decisions still to be made. My sister is quiet in the backseat.

After we park and head for the elevator, Brooke asks, "Flowers?"

"I'm going to look. Tomorrow maybe?" I say, fumbling for my phone.

"I can go with you," Brooke offers.

"I thought you had to go out of town?" I say to my friend.

"I can cancel."

My gaze flicks to my sister, guilt rising up. Brooke has a way of knowing what looks fantastic together, and she always has my back, but I'm worried about Mari. "Mar? Can you help me with flowers?"

"I suppose."

"Great." When my friend's face falls, I add, "Brooke, can you help with the venue later this week?"

"Absolutely."

All my life, I wanted people to love and accept me. Now, having two people I care about clamoring to be there...

I'll remind them they're both important to me.

We head inside the condo, and the beautiful brightness of the open space greets us.

During our short stint in LA, I found us a house to rent. After returning to Denver the next season, it made sense to return to the condo Clay purchased when he first signed with the Kodiaks. It's objectively beautiful, but it's never felt like mine, and now that I'm keeping busy with painting and Clay's starting to set down roots, we're running out of room.

I have my rented studio in the city where I can paint, but sometimes it would be nice to have some space to spread out at home. The second bedroom of the condo is a jumbled mass of paperwork, Clay's trophies and awards, and my painting stuff.

The wine fridge in the kitchen isn't as impressive as Mari and Harlan's walk-in basement wine cellar, but there's no champagne inside.

I open the cupboard and find a foil-covered bottle of Moet. "How's this?"

"If that's all you have," Mari says.

"It's not about the brand. It's about the quality," Brooke weighs in.

"It's also warm," Mari counters.

Brooke shrugs. "Hand it over."

She grabs a towel to open the champagne and my attention drifts to the photos on the wall. There's a selfie of Clay and me in Aruba, his tattooed arms circling me from behind as we lie on the beach. Another of the Kodiaks crowded around their booth at Mile High. One of Mari and me as kids wearing flower crowns and dancing in a field.

Finally, there's one of Clay and Kat, both of

them kids and dressed in footie pajamas, their parents behind them. They're not terribly close to Clay and Kat, and I've only met them twice on video calls.

Still, according to Clay, they were always supportive of his basketball growing up—almost to a fault. They live on the East Coast and occasionally go to his games if he's nearby.

Mari's words come back to me. *Being a wife is different from being a girlfriend.*

Why should it be? We've been together for two years, and in that time, we've faced countless challenges and come out stronger.

My gaze focuses on a selfie we took at Red Rocks, Clay holding me and both of us grinning into the camera.

"This stupid bottle..." Brooke's cursing from the kitchen pulls my attention back. She wrestles with the cork.

"Here, pass it to me," Mari says.

They start wrestling with the bottle, and finally I step between them. "Let's try something different... AHHH!"

The cork flies off, and the champagne erupts in a violent stream of bubbly sugar and alcohol. It covers my face, my dress, my hair, and half the kitchen.

Brooke and Mari's expressions slacken in shock.

I pour myself a glass from the half-empty bottle and take a sip. "This is pretty good." I laugh, and they do too.

I pour two more glasses and we toast.

"To my sister," Mari says.

"And my friend," Brooke jumps in.

I push a chunk of sticky hair out of my face as I take a long drink. The doorbell buzzes, and I skip, barefoot, across the marble floor.

"Clay's shoes!" I toss over my shoulder by way of an explanation.

The doorman would usually call up, but I told him to send wedding stuff up directly to make life easier for him.

Downing the rest of the champagne, I bounce toward the hallway with the empty glass still in one hand. Pale yellow champagne streaks my cream dress, and my pink hair sticks to my face and neck.

The delivery guy will forgive me.

"I know the shoes are huge," I call through the door, the taste of wine giving me a happy buzz and making everything feel that much better, "but you should see the rest of..."

I yank on the handle, and the door swings wide. Standing in the open doorway are a man and woman. My smile fades as shock replaces the laughter.

"... him," I finish. My free hand forms a sticky fist as I recognize the people from the photo on the wall, dressed impeccably and surveying my disheveled state.

Clay's parents.

7

NOVA

"I'm so thrilled you made it to Denver." I paste on a smile as I look up at Clay's mother. "And so quickly."

And when I was covered in champagne.

Five minutes ago, I insisted Mari and Brooke could go, promising I had this under control. Now, Clay's parents are installed on opposite armchairs.

They're both taller than I expected, probably because I've only seen them standing next to him in pictures.

"Let me get you a drink," I say, partly to be a good host and also to give myself a minute to regroup.

When Clay and I sat down with the

wedding planner, we talked about the bare minimum of guests. She'd asked about my parents, at which point I said they'd passed. She asked about Clay's, and he said they might come but not to plan a special role for them.

But now they're here. Days ahead of time.

In the kitchen, there's still a glass worth of champagne, but that's probably bad luck. I pull out a bottle of red. And another of white.

"How was your flight?" I ask.

"Dry air. Too crowded, even in first class."

Clay's parents are, he's implied, successful. His father, Thomas, runs his own company. He's confident and assured in the way fifty-something men in suits can be. His mother, Sandy, is slim with honey-blond hair cut in a sleek bob.

"Which do you prefer?" I ask, holding up both bottles.

"Sparkling water would be lovely for both of us," Sandy replies, barely glancing at the wine.

"Right." I return to the kitchen and pull open the fridge door. No luck.

When I bring Clay's mother tap water, her lips thin. She and her husband are perched in chairs like matching bookends. I take a seat on the couch.

"We're so glad you could be here," I say.

"Our only son tells us he's planning to get married," Thomas says dryly. "We took the first flight."

"Planning to," not "is getting married." Did he mean to make it sound as if our minds – Clay's mind—might still be changed?

I'm sure he didn't.

All parents want is to know how loved their children are. So, that's what I'm going to show them.

"It was so nice to speak with you at the holidays and after finals. Clay talks about you all the time."

It's a bit of a fib, but it's in the spirit of family, so I don't think my fiancé would mind.

"Really? Last year was the first time we'd heard about you," Sandy says.

My smile dies.

We make small talk for a few minutes, but it feels like playing a game by myself. Every time I start a topic, I have to carry it on.

The sound of the door opening makes me leap up with hope.

Clay enters, wearing gray jogging pants with a hat pulled over his head and a gear bag slung over his shoulder.

"Clayton, darling," his mother gushes.

My brows shoot up to my hairline. I've never heard anyone be ooey-gooey around Clay before. It's not what I expect him to go for, or even tolerate. But he looks surprisingly relaxed as his gaze flicks between us once as his parents rise and embrace him, his father coming up to Clay's chin and his mother barely reaching his chest.

"Could I borrow you for a minute?" I say once they're finished greeting one another.

Clay follows me to the bedroom, where I carefully shut the door behind us.

"Did you know they were coming?" I fight to keep my voice low enough they can't hear from the other room.

"Not tonight." He sets his bag on the bed and rubs a hand through his hair.

"But you're happy they're here," I press. Clay keeps his emotions under wraps, even sometimes with me, and I want to be there for him.

"We decided to have the wedding here in part so we could include family and friends."

He's right.

I don't have a lot of family, and these people made Clay who he is. I want to win them over.

I square my shoulders. "Then they should stay for dinner."

Clay's brows rise under the fall of his hair. "Dinner," he echoes.

"Yes. I want to get to know them. I'll order from that restaurant we like." I flash a confident smile.

I'll convince them this is the best idea ever. If Clay loves them, I will too.

"Had ten promotional offers in the last month," Clay finishes. "My agent bought two new Maseratis this year thanks to me."

Tom is on the edge of his seat.

Sandy clasps her hands as she leans in. "Clayton, that's wonderful. You deserve that and more."

His father nods. "You'll have more offers this year and for years to come."

After Clay arrived, I excused myself to go change and call our new favorite restaurant to see if they could deliver dinner. Unsure of what they wanted, I ordered a couple servings of everything.

Now, seated at the table with too much food, it's a lovefest, and Clay's at the center of it. He seems genuinely oblivious, as though he's talking about what happened at the office today.

"Defending a championship's tough, but we're trying to enjoy the challenge. Especially given I'm not sure how long I'll be playing basketball."

His mother's manicured brows lift. "Whatever do you mean?"

Clay meets my eyes. "Can't play pro forever."

My heart kicks. I love him for saying that out loud. It's been a point of struggle for him, realizing he'll have to do something else one day.

"Come on, Clayton," his dad says. "They have ways of extending careers these days.

Surgeries. Bench roles. This is what you were born for. You're a gladiator," his dad says. "You were forged for battle."

"Gladiators died young," I point out. "I'd rather Clay enjoy himself long after his career is over than deal with the fallout from too many injuries."

Every eye settles on me.

"What is it you do for work?" Clay's father asks in a way that makes me wonder if there's a right answer.

"I'm an artist. I paint, mostly."

"Nova's been commissioned to do lots of important pieces," Clay says. Pride rises up, and gratitude for him speaking up for me. "Her first big job was at the Kodiaks stadium."

"It was good of you to facilitate that," his mom says.

He didn't.

I squeeze my glass and cut a look at Clay, trying not to seem desperate. Winning them over is proving harder than I thought.

Maybe once they see how committed we are to the wedding, to each other, they'll get on board.

"Let us tell you about the ceremony and the reception," I try.

Clay nods subtly, an encouragement.

I launch into an explanation the venue and the plans, and his mother listens between sips of water as she nibbles her chicken.

"Only thirty people? Surely that's not your entire guest list." She looks between us. "Clayton, you have extended family. Thousands of people who know you and value your career."

"We don't want a crowd," he says.

"What about a prenup?"

My water goes down the wrong way. I cough, sputtering.

"You okay?" Clays brows pull together.

"Perfect," I manage.

I'm itching for another glass of wine. I'll wring it out of my stained dress if I have to.

8

———

CLAY

I haven't watched the clock so hard since the final seconds of the championship game.

It's nearly eleven when they leave. After I shut the door behind them, my mom pressing a kiss in the general direction of my cheek, I lean back against the door to take in the damage. Nova's sitting on the couch, arms folded, staring off into space.

My girl is a lot of things, but naturally silent isn't one of them.

"So, that's them," I say to break the stillness.

I'm worried them showing up was too much for her, if I fucked up by not realizing they'd come straight here. She's good with people, but my parents can be a lot.

She blows out a breath. "You guys seem closer than I expected."

"Meaning what?" I cross to her and sink onto the couch, the cushion creaking under my weight.

"They're very...invested."

The last thing I want to do is let my parents' visit cause problems for us. But navigating interpersonal family stuff is not my go to move. Hell, it's not in my top ten.

"Getting your kid to go pro isn't easy. They dedicated time, money, all of it from when I was this tall." I lift my hand to my knee. "Drove me to tournaments. Got the best coaching, the best camps. Spare bedroom of our house was full of shoes and gear by the time I was ten. They're proud of what I've accomplished."

"And they should be, Clay." Her eyes soften. "Their son is everything a parent could hope for. Dedicated. Kind. Caring."

Of course, she doesn't mention that I'm a legend on the court. One more thing I love about her.

"Come here. Turn around," I say.

"Huh?"

"Do it."

Nova swivels, and I inch closer, my hands taking her small shoulders and massaging circles.

"Ohh. That's good." Her voice lowers, and my lips curve.

That's what I want. Her relaxing.

"How was your day?" I ask.

"I found a dress."

My thumbs still.

"Did you take pictures?"

"Yes."

My attention scans the room until I see her phone on the coffee table.

"Don't even think about it," she warns.

I lunge for the phone. She's on my heels, but she's no match for a pro athlete. I snatch up the device and rise, swiping the bar to open it.

"You don't know my password!" she says as she grabs at my arms, one arm looping halfway around my waist.

"It's my birthday." The digits get typed in, the screen flashing red.

She replies, "Maybe I changed it."

"To what?"

Nova folds her arms, tipping her little chin up at me. "My other fiancé's birthday?"

I groan. "Careful, Pink. I'll have to show you exactly how much you're mine."

I want to see this dress, and I'm used to getting my way. But every battle requires different tactics. Mostly I play ones on the court, but now I need to try something new.

My voice lowers. "Tell me what it's like."

Nova's lips press together, but there's a sparkle in her eyes I haven't seen all night. "What it's like..."

I step closer, the phone forgotten as I reach for her waist. "Is it white? Long? Puffy? Shiny?" I bend my lips to her ear, and she arches toward me.

She's wearing jeans and a soft sweater that, since my parents left, is now falling temptingly off one shoulder. Her hair skims her creamy skin, and I want to drag a finger along her collarbone until she makes that breathy little hiccup that says she can't resist me.

"No," she whispers stubbornly.

"No, it's not any of those? You're going to walk to the altar naked."

A little laugh. "No, I'm not telling you."

Fuck, she's cute.

"I'll get it out of you."

"You can try," she replies pleasantly.

"Pink, I'm the best offensive player in the league."

Her nose wrinkles. "You're top three."

The words hit like an elbow to the chest, knocking the wind from me. I recover enough to draw a ragged breath. "Sweetheart, you don't mean that."

She flips her palms. "I'm only saying what the stats guys say..."

Oh, it's on.

"The stats guys aren't here to save you," I growl as I back her against the wall and hitch her legs up around me. Her ankles hook around my waist, my fingers digging into the soft flesh of her ass.

Nova laughs, but her eyes widen with apprehension. "What are you going to do?"

"Make you wish you'd told me the first time."

My fingers skim down her ribcage...

And I tickle.

"NOOOO!" she shrieks.

In this moment, I'm grateful to Kat, who

told me eyes don't get stuck in the back of your head no matter how hard you roll them.

"Tell me."

Again, she twists in my arms, screeching. "I won't, that would ruin it!"

Doesn't she know nothing in this world could ruin the sight of her walking toward me about to become my wife?

Not if she was naked.

Or in my jersey.

Both of which have starred in my fantasies.

"Stop it!" she pants through her desperate laughter. She arches, her muscles flexing and exposing her soft throat.

I feel victory looming on the horizon. I bend toward her and kiss a trail down her smooth skin, frowning when I taste a hit of sugar. "You taste... sweet."

She flushes, the color painting her skin almost as pink as her hair. "Brooke, Mari, and I were celebrating when your parents came over. The champagne exploded on me and I was a total mess and rushed to change." Her voice creeps higher with every syllable, as though she's confessing to a crime. "There's half a bottle still open in the kitchen."

I'm so close to getting the information I want. She's about to wave the white flag.

Except...

She wanted to celebrate with her girls and didn't get to. Today was supposed to be her time.

"Come on." I lead the way to the kitchen. When we get there, I lift her to perch on the edge of the dining table. She eyes me with one brow arched. I tug up her shirt to expose more sweet skin that I run my lips over. "We didn't have dessert."

Nova shivers, her blue eyes widening with anticipation and surprise.

She's beautiful. More than that, she's cheerful and bright like a rainbow no matter what's happening around her. I'm in awe of her. I won't let anything put out her smile.

I retrieve the bottle, plus a clean champagne flute.

When I return and she sees what's in my hands, her eyes widen. I set the bottle and flute on the table.

"What's that for?" she asks.

I pour the glass, then hold it out to her. "You."

Her eyes soften as she takes a sip. "It's better from the glass," she decides with a contended sigh.

"You're wrong about that."

I shoot her a wicked look before I grab the hem of her shirt and strip it off over her head in a single motion. Under it, she's wearing a pink lace bra, her nipples peeking through the fabric.

I take the glass back and tip it over her exposed stomach. A river runs into her navel, making her gasp.

"Clay—!"

I bend over her and press my mouth to her stomach, sucking out the champagne. The taste is sweetness mixed with her, and I want to compare that flavor to every other inch of her.

She bites her lip, face flushed as she watches.

"Don't move," I command as I drag her jeans down her hips. The scrap of lace remaining matches her bra and makes me a new kind of feral.

"Spread your legs, Pink. I want dessert."

She bites her lip but does what I say. I reach for the champagne flute.

"You wouldn't..."

I hook a finger in the panel of her thong and yank it to the side so I can pour champagne over her pussy. I follow it with my fingers, the stickiness of the wine mixing with her arousal.

I want to suck every drop off her skin.

My eyes hold hers prisoner as I lower my mouth.

The second I lick her, she arches against my tongue with a breathy moan.

"Oh my God."

Her fingers grip my hair, desperation in her grasp.

My fiancée and I have a game when I'm going down on her.

I know she likes how much bigger I am than her, and I don't hate it either.

How full I make her just from my fingers, the way she squirms on me to tell me I'm on the right track.

I'm going to put everything from earlier out of her beautiful head.

There are perks to being my wife.

I'll remind her all fucking night of them.

I enjoy teasing her with my tongue, adding another finger until she can't take any more.

"Dammit, don't we have a safe word?" she pants.

"You want me to stop?"

"Don't you dare."

I pull back long enough to yank my shirt over my head with one hand. She's already dragging off my sweats.

I brace a hand next to her head and shift over her. If I put my full weight on this table, it could break. But when my cock finds its home between her spread thighs, she feels too damned good to go easy.

I sink inside, and the feel of her body's welcome and resistance at once makes me shudder. She's tight and slick and mine.

I thrust long and slow, the rhythm making us both groan. The lights overhead send gold sparks dancing in her eyes.

"You feel fucking perfect," I murmur against her throat.

Damn, I want only her, like this, for hours.

She arches into my lips, my body. Her need fuels mine.

I change the angle to get more friction and grind against her clit, the way I know drives her wild.

"Oh God, Clay," she whispers.

I grin against her shoulder. My lips skim her skin as I inhale the scent of her, of us together.

The city on the other side of the dining room windows is a million dots of color, the mountains invisible in the low light. All I care about is what's happening in here.

Nova's gasping, approaching an invisible edge I know by her sounds, her feel, the way her fingers dig into my shoulders.

She tightens around me, her collarbone damp with sweat as she arches, eyes closed in pleasure.

Watching her come is too much. There's no way I can witness her giving herself to me like that without reciprocating. It's like asking a man to resist breathing.

My muscles clench and I come inside her, shuddering out the last of my need.

"This is the most fun I've had at this table tonight," she says when we can speak again.

I pull back an inch to look at her, smug. "Only tonight?"

Her fingers trail along my arm. "Let's just stay here a minute."

I pull her against me so our sweaty skin is flush.

"How was practice?" she asks.

I think about the mayor stopping by to talk with James. The lack of progress finding the perfect house.

"Not as good as this," I say honestly.

Her lips curve, and I swear I see my happiness in this woman's face every damn time.

"We should do some wedding planning tonight," Nova murmurs.

I nuzzle into her neck. "That's what we're doing."

"How do you figure?" Suspicion has her pulling back.

"I'm planning for our wedding night."

The next round, I roll her on top.

9

———

CLAY

Four days until the wedding

"**G**o hard. Like a lion. A tiger. A shark."

The passionate requests sound oddly dry in the photographer's British accent.

I'm wearing my Kodiaks uniform and shoes, but there's no court in sight, only a setup of lights flashing white and gold over our mini-set in the basement studio at the stadium.

"Faster," he urges as his flash clicks away. "Now turn. I want more of these feral tattoos."

I slide a look toward Chloe, who's bent over her iPad in one corner and fighting the urge to roll her eyes.

This shoot was a late addition to my calendar. Though we normally have our share of team commitments heading into the season, this was an unwelcome distraction.

Not least because something's eating Nova.

Touching her last night—holding her, giving us both a release—took the edge off physically, but even as we fell asleep, she wasn't totally relaxed.

My parents showing up early, and unannounced, was a surprise. I reminded my fiancée she doesn't need to cater to them, particularly given she's thrown herself into planning what was supposed to be an easy, low-key wedding.

Remembering Kat's words, I texted my mom this morning to remind her to be nice to Nova. She promised she would and insisted any shortness last night was in my imagination.

"How much longer?" I ask Chloe as I assume an aggressive stance, turned sideways to the camera, my fists clenched.

Click-click. Click-click.

Her eyes don't move from her phone. "Twenty minutes?"

I told Nova I'd be done by mid-morning and ready to help with any wedding tasks the rest of the day. It's already nearly lunch.

"Who's in after me?" Maybe I can tap out faster if the next Kodiaks player is ready to go.

"No one."

I straighten instantly. "Chlo, what aren't you telling me?"

Her brows lift, her lips working for a moment before she says the words. "This is for the mayor's office."

"The mayor's office doesn't need promo photos. They can use the team's."

Chloe blinks at me. "Well, they asked for them, and apparently you said you'd act as ambassador."

Dammit.

She's got me there.

"Five more minutes," I concede.

"You have one more costume change." She holds up a bag.

"The fuck is this?" I grunt.

"Special city-edition uniform."

Behind a divider in the corner, I change into the all-gold jersey. I drag on the shorts, taking a look at the front of the jersey before I pull it on. There's a shiny purple bear on it with "Kodiaks" in shiny, slanted letters.

"Feel like the Wizard of fucking Oz," I grumble as I shrug into it.

As I emerge, Chloe reaches behind her seat and comes out with a basketball, which she throws at me hard enough that I have to react quickly to catch it.

"Thanks for being a team player." Her smile is wide.

Once the five minutes is up, I change, stalk out of the studio, and head toward the exit and send a text on the way.

Clay: On my way, Pink. I'm ready to be put to work.

When I pass the gym, my gaze catches on the guys inside. Miles is benching, Rookie spotting him. The weight on the barbell impresses even me.

"What've you been eating?" I ask as I stick my head in.

"More than cappuccinos," Miles grunts as he finishes a rep, the barbell clanging into its cups. He sits up and swipes a towel across his face.

"He's going to be a beast this year," Rookie claims.

"What does that make you?"

"Baby beast," Miles says, and Rookie shoves his shoulder hard enough that Miles coughs.

Rookie crosses to the cooler to refill his water as the text from Nova comes back.

Nova: Hey, I'm actually going to meet up with Mari right now.

Nova: Tomorrow I'm going for a fitting, but I was planning to drop by the venue after to go over logistics at 2p.m. Want to come with?

My realtor sent a new list of prospective properties this morning on my way to practice, including one that looks promising. But, he said we can't get in to see it until tomorrow afternoon.

Clay: I've got a conflict after lunch. I could be there closer to four?

Dots appear, then stop.

Nova: Don't worry about it. I've got it under control.

I frown. She's got it under control like it's not important? Or like she doesn't want me to show at all?

Suddenly I'm second guessing my plans.

"I know that look," Miles calls. "That's a girl-problem look."

Rookie snorts. "Don't tell me you're having second thoughts."

"We're not. Everything's fine."

The guys are at my shoulders reading the screen before I can think to hide it.

"See?" I say, nodding to the text. "She says it's fine."

Rookie covers his face with a hand. Miles coughs, shaking his head.

"Sure it's fine, bro."

NOVA

"Is it poisoned?"

I lift my head, raising a brow at Mari across the table in my studio downtown.

"Your coffee." She nods toward my cup. "You've barely taken a sip."

"Not unless Clay's mother made it for me," I grumble.

We're reviewing the flower arrangements for the wedding sent over by the planner. I wanted simple, but she suggested decorating the altar and lining the aisle in addition to a large bouquet for me.

Around us are stacks of fresh canvases, plus a few pieces that are in between homes.

"It can't be that bad," Mari says.

"Sandy hates me." I shove a piece of hair out of my face.

Mari leans on one elbow, frowning. "She doesn't know you."

I take a long drink of coffee, which is now closer to iced than warm. "I'm trying," I say after I fill her in on last night's dinner from hell. "This morning, I texted to ask if I could show her around Denver. I sent two cases of sparkling water to her hotel. Nothing. Clay said his dad will work while he's here, but so far, his mom's main job is avoiding me."

"It's probably natural that she's having a hard time letting go of her only son."

I spread my hands. "Letting go?! It's not as if I'm taking him anywhere."

Mari's lips twitch. "You were never this tidy growing up," she comments as she catches me looking at one of the stacks.

"It's called inventory," I inform her.

"What are we putting in the reception room?" she asks. Her gaze lowers to the documents we're reviewing from the planner. My sister's better at detailed stuff and planning than I am.

"I haven't even thought about the reception yet."

Mari pulls up photos of the space on her laptop. "We can bring the flowers from the ceremony inside, put them around the space on the tables here and here." She points. "But it's not going to be enough. Outdoors, there's the backdrop of nature. Here, there's a vast hall that will drown us out."

I rise from my seat and pace my studio,

weaving between the neat stacks of white canvas stretched onto frames.

Mari flips through the single stack of completed canvases, pausing on one in particular. "Nova, what's this?"

I peer over her shoulder. There are swooshing lines of pink and purple. "Flowers. But in abstract."

"I bet it felt good to make it."

My fingertips tingle with the memory. "It did."

I've been so focused on the wedding and the upcoming season, my art has taken a backseat. But I've been experimenting with flower designs lately, and seeing them once more makes me light up with purpose.

Mari retrieves a blank canvas from my collection of them and a fresh jar of water.

"We need to work on decor for the wedding," I point out.

"The bride needs to relax," she counters.

It's a standoff. Until she grabs a second canvas, setting it up on a spare easel back-to-back with mine.

"Do it with me." Mari's dressed for an outing, not for painting.

"You're really going to paint?" I eye her skeptically. "When was the last time you made something?"

"Probably third grade." She grins. "I'll put the drycleaning on the bride's tab."

I rummage through my drawer of brushes to find another and hold it out.

We paint facing one another, the easels between us. The rhythm sucks me in, and I lose myself to the colors and the shapes.

When I'm here, it feels as if I'm where I'm supposed to be. There are no one's expectations, including my own. Nobody to tell me what I should or shouldn't or can or can't.

I don't realize what time it is until Mari's phone buzzes and she reaches for it.

"Harlan asking if I'll be home before he leaves. Emily's finished dinner, and he has to go out for a team meeting in an hour."

"Wow. I can't believe we were here for three hours." Outside the window, the sky is dimming with dusk.

"Can I see it?" I ask.

She bites her lip, then motions me over. What I see takes my breath away.

"That's beautiful, Mar," I say, leaning an elbow on her shoulder.

"What about yours?"

I grab my canvas and bring it around, holding it up next to hers. We've used the same shades of purple and pink, and similar brushstrokes.

"They're so similar," she murmurs, hovering a finger over the canvas. "Not that I know what I'm doing."

"You did great."

"If only decorating the venue was this easy," she says.

An idea strikes me.

"What if it is?" I lift both canvases, careful not to touch the wet fronts, and hold them up against the white walls. "These would look amazing in the hall."

Her expression brightens with delight. "We'd need more. Two."

The idea of having pieces we created together thrills me, but reality comes crashing in.

"When would we have time?" I ask.

She has to get home. Her responsibilities are different than mine.

Mari taps her lip, and for a moment, she looks like me. "Right now. Emily's nanny can put her to bed. I'll say good night when I get home."

My arms go around my sister before I can think. "You're the best sometimes."

She hugs me back. "Only sometimes?"

10

CLAY

By the time I tap out for the day, it's after six.

With Nova ditching me, I called the realtor to see what he could show me on short notice. Figured if I found the perfect place today, it'd have the bonus of freeing me up tomorrow so I could go to Aspen with her.

We visited three houses. Nothing was a fit.

One was too small. Another didn't have a view of the mountains. The third I couldn't put my finger on what was wrong, but I couldn't picture Nova dancing through the kitchen on Saturday morning in her bunny slippers, and that was reason enough for me.

I'm used to having all the answers.

Especially if the question can be answered with money. It's frustrating as hell.

Instead of pulling up in the parking garage of my building, I find myself in front of the team's bar. Mile High has grown on me over the past couple of years. Not only because I'm a part owner, but because it's the kind of spot where I immediately feel at ease no matter how rough my day was.

I'm barely inside the front doors when the bartender calls, "Clay!"

"I need a drink and a corner where no one will bother me."

"Corners we've got." Sierra grins.

She turns away, returning a moment later with two glasses. One contains water, the other a frothy amber liquid that definitely isn't water.

"Season hasn't started yet," she points out.

"Week and a half." But I take a sip of the beer. "Your dad around?"

Not because I'm looking for company, but I should at least say hello. It's been a minute since I was here, and as a forty-nine-percent owner of the place, I try to check in.

"He's taking a vacation. But don't worry, he'll be home for opening night."

"Surprised you could get him out of here for more than a couple shifts."

"I gave him an ultimatum. He left me with the place for a week, or I wouldn't come back." Her gaze lifts behind me. "To what do I owe the pleasure?"

"Bear sense," Miles calls. "We knew Clay was drinking and figured we'd come celebrate."

I turn to see half the team filing through the door. *So much for alone time.*

Jay reaches me first, hands shoved in the pockets of his college basketball team jacket as he sits on the stool next to me. "Haven't had a proper toast for you and Nova with everything going on."

Hanging with the entire team wasn't what I had in mind tonight. It's hard to brood in a group.

But they're not leaving.

"For real. It's easy to get caught up in basketball, but life passes us by," Jay insists.

"This is a big deal," Atlas says in his gravelly voice.

"Plus, we got the invites and have so many questions," Miles adds.

Their faces are earnest.

Fuck. It's like having family. You push 'em away, but they won't stay gone.

I nod to Sierra to bring a round for the guys.

When the drinks arrive, the guys raise their glasses.

Rookie jumps in first. "This one's for Clay. You taught me that being a pro is about actions, not words."

Atlas smacks him lightly on the back of the head. "Whatever, Keats."

"Who's throwing your bachelor party?" Jay asks. "And Nova's bachelorette?"

"No one. Because we're not having them."

I've been to my share of bachelor parties with varying degrees of cringe. It's not on my priority list.

"We have to do one. No arguing," says Jay.

"I'm the best party planner," Miles says.

"Nah, I'll do it. You can be my second," Jay cuts in.

"Just like on the court," Rookie whispers.

"Is there anything I can say to get you to drop this?" I ask.

They exchange a look. "Nah," they chorus.

If only they could agree to anything that easily on the court.

"Fine," I relent, and a cheer goes up.

Maybe it'll be good to have the bonding before the start of the season.

"Just be smart," I say. "Season's starting in a few days."

"No strippers or coke," Miles translates.

"Or skydiving or streaking," Jay finishes.

Rookie looks between us. "That what you usually have at your parties?"

"Course not," Atlas snorts. "Not the coke anyway."

Miles stands up. "I'll rock-paper-scissors you for it."

He and Jay square off.

First time, they both pull scissors.

Then rock.

"Not real academic types," Atlas says in my ear.

A few more draws and Miles pulls paper over Jay's rock.

Miles crows with victory. "Like you said, Jay—you run things on the court. I'm running this."

Jay frowns, looking for a way to argue, but there's nothing he can do.

"Why'd you fight for this?" I ask Miles.

"You do a lot for us. I want to return the favor."

I'm not the kind of guy to lean on other people, but they make it impossible not to care about them.

When our round is done, the guys are laughing about something when Sierra leans over. "Another?"

I shake my head.

"Call Nova," Jay says. "It's damn obvious you want to."

Rejection is always close at hand, but Nova's never given me reason to feel like I can't put myself on the line with her.

I lift the phone and hit her contact.

Three rings, then her voicemail chirps. "This is Nova. I'm so glad you called!"

Her voice makes my chest tighten. The pleasure at her cheeriness blurs with disappointment that she's still dodging me.

"Hey, Pink. It's me. I'm at Mile High with the guys and heading home in an hour or so." I pause. "I miss you."

I click off and turn back to the guys.

We're getting ready to leave when I feel a tapping on my shoulder.

I turn to find Nova standing behind me, dressed in a denim jacket, her hair piled up in a loose knot.

"Pink."

"Sorry I missed your call. Mari and I were painting at the studio." Her lips curve as she reaches up to play with a piece of hair that's fallen out of her bun.

My mood that's been getting darker all night lifts, like clouds blown through on a breeze.

"It's all good. I'm glad you came."

Relief edges in at the confirmation that she wasn't purposely avoiding me.

She greets the guys warmly, exchanging hugs.

"Congrats," Miles murmurs.

"It's going to be epic," Rookie agrees.

"We're gonna go." Once everyone's done

saying hi, Jay hitches a thumb toward the door. "Have a good night, kids."

Nova shifts onto a stool next to me once the guys are headed for the door.

Sierra brings Nova a cocktail, and she accepts it.

"Tell me what's going on," I prod.

"Just the usual wedding stuff. Brooke and Mari are both stepping up to help. They've turned it into a competitive sport."

"Need a referee?"

"Thanks." Nova's smile lights up the entire room. "Mostly, I'm glad to be this loved. How about you?"

I don't want to tell her about the house until it's a done deal.

"Nothing but chill." I squeeze her hand, and she laughs.

"You could spend the next season in cold storage and you wouldn't come out chill."

Now we're both grinning.

Mile High is quiet tonight. It's midweek, and there are some regulars who give us space. Only the odd person glances over in a way that lingers more than a second or two.

"Do you think we'd be good parents?" she asks.

I turn it over, surprised by the change in subject. But the way she asks makes me give the question the same consideration I always do. "Yeah. I think we would. What made you ask that?"

"I was thinking about kids and parents today. It's obvious how much yours love you."

The way her voice trembles at the edge, I know she's thinking of her own parents.

I want to protect this girl from the world. But I can't take that back, can't change the tragedy. At least she doesn't blame herself anymore for not being on that plane with them.

I couldn't handle living in this world without Nova by my side. Now that I know she exists, no day is as bright without her.

I swivel on my stool to face her, resting a foot on the rungs on either side of her feet. Her face is open when I lift her chin, making the lights over the bar shine on her bright blue eyes, her parted lips. "You're caring and kind. You see people at their best and love them at their worst. There's no one I'd picture having kids with other than you."

Her eyes shine, the corners getting damp. I take her face in my hands and brush the tears away with my thumbs.

"Sometimes I wonder how I got so selfish," I murmur. "I feel lucky with what I've done in my life so far. I've seen things, been part of things, a lot of people never will. But there are so many more things I want to do and be. They're all since I met you."

The tears are back, but her lips are curved. She nudges me away and tries to swipe at them with the sleeve of her sweater. I bring her face back and kiss her.

"I want everything with you, Nova," I murmur against her mouth.

Her arms wind around my neck as she kisses me back. It's a knot I never want to untie.

"I want that too," she whispers.

I brush my fingers across her knuckles. The ring I gave her is smooth under my thumb. Knowing it's my ring on her finger is a kind of satisfaction I never expected.

When she looks at me with curiosity, I explain, "Feels good."

Her hands twine with mine, and I feel her rub my ring finger.

"One more week and I'll know for sure," she murmurs back.

It's like a hit to my chest. "You want to put a ring on me?"

"More than anything." Her lips curve.

Fuck. This girl has all of me.

She's seen the darkest parts of me, and she's still here, looking at me as though I'm it for her.

"You two need anything?" Sierra asks from somewhere in my peripheral vision.

Nova's eyes move over mine, her gaze bright and a million miles deep.

"Nothing," I reply.

My legs straddle hers, and I want to be alone with her almost as much as I want to never move from this place. No matter what happens this week with basketball or the house or my parents, we have this.

We have us.

11

NOVA

Three days until the wedding

"Jay Z and Beyoncé." I stab my finger in the air.

"No." Brooke tosses her hair as she cuts me a look from the driver's seat.

"Posh and David Beckham?"

This time, I get a sigh. "No."

My face screws up. "Snoop Dogg?"

"He's not married. Dammit, Nova, I said famous people have gotten married here, but you're not taking this guessing game at all seriously." Brooke slaps a palm against the steering wheel of her car.

Brooke wanted to help me go over the venue arrangements with the planner. I'm glad to have the help, though partly this feels like making up for Mari hanging with me yesterday.

I remember how I felt when I came to Mari's wedding and learned she'd picked Chloe as MOH over me. It wasn't about a role—it was about closeness. It had seemed like we weren't as close as I thought we were.

Which is why even though we decided not to have bridal parties, I'm reminding Brooke she's my closest friend.

She parks and we get out, retrieving four huge squares wrapped in white.

"These are very mysterious," she comments as we carry the packages up to the resort.

Brooke and I meet the wedding planner at the reception desk.

First, she takes us to the reception area. "Then we'll head out to the deck," she suggests as she escorts us through the room. "We'll have it laid out with round tables seating eight. You didn't want a head table, so the equivalent will seat"—she consults her list—"the bride and groom, groom's parents, groom's sister and partner, and bride's sister and brother-in-law."

"That sounds right," I say.

"I'll send you the layout when we finish," she promises, resting a hand on the back of one chair. She gestures to a long, narrow area next to the tables. "This area is for dancing."

"It's not enough room," Brooke says. "There's barely—"

Barking interrupts her, and a little dog bolts across the rich carpet and throws himself onto Brooke's sheer patterned tights.

"Hi, handsome!" Brooke croons as she scoops up Waffles. "Tell me I'm wrong about this layout," she challenges the furry face licking at hers.

"You're wrong about the layout." An amused male voice comes from behind us.

Miles leans against the doorway in faded jeans and a navy zip-up sweater that makes his eyes look the color of the sky on a sunny day. His hair sticks up as if he drove a convertible the entire way here.

Knowing Miles, maybe he did.

"Wasn't talking to you," Brooke tosses lightly, cuddling the dog closer.

Miles narrows his eyes at the dog.

Waffles makes a little whine, ducking to rub his face against Brooke's shoulder.

"What are you doing here?" I ask as I unwrap the first canvas.

Miles's expression, the lopsided grin on his handsome face, immediately puts me at ease. "Clay thought you might need help doing a walk-through of the venue. Guy's busy with... his stuff."

"Stuff?" Brooke and I say in unison, exchanging a look.

Miles backtracks. "Err... nothing important."

A twinge of disappointment rises up.

Last night after painting with Mari, I went to find Clay at Mile High. Being close to him always makes me feel more grounded. But I'm not ready to admit that things aren't clicking with the people who raised him. It feels as if we should be close, or at least that we should all understand one another.

"The venue is under control," Brooke

informs him. "But if we need someone to make coffees, we'll let you know."

He scoffs, feigning wounded.

A couple of girls stick their heads into the room, their eyes purely on Miles. "Hey, are you...?"

I tune them out as they gush over Miles. He turns his back on us as if to say, "If you don't want my attention, someone else does."

Brooke gives Waffles one last kiss before she sets him back on the carpet. He makes a little sound of protest, as though he'd rather be in her arms again, but she's already crossing to me. "Those are really pretty."

"Thanks. Mari and I made them last night."

She folds her arms, her lips pressing together.

I finish unwrapping one and hold it up. "I'm glad you're here today."

Brooke nods, her smile back in place. "Of course. We're friends. You know that."

The click of a camera phone and some tinkling laughter has me glancing over to see Miles nod at the girls. They leave, clearly reluctant, and he turns back to us.

"Clay tell you I'm working on an epic plan for his bachelor party?" he asks casually.

"I'm shocked you'd have time around tending to your fan club," Brooke says.

Miles doesn't take the bait. "I make time for what's important."

"What are you planning?"

"Top secret."

"Whatever it is, it's not as good as Nova's bachelorette," Brooke counters.

I don't have time to respond before Miles jumps in. "When's that?"

"Ahhh..." Brooke trails off.

"Clay's is tomorrow."

"So's Nova's," Brooke says.

I lower the canvas I'm holding. I was looking forward to a couple of nights with Clay before all the excitement of the wedding and the season. I wish he had told me last night about a bachelor party.

"It's a rite of passage," Brooke says, reading my expression. "One last night of being free."

Maybe that will be the perfect time to reassure Brooke and Mari I love them both and that this will be fun for everyone.

"Sounds amazing," I decide. "Just let me try these pictures out for placement."

"Right. Where did the wedding planner go? I need to talk to her about the dancing space. It's the wrong shape. It should be a square." She motions with her hands. "As it is, it's way too narrow and long."

Michael Bublé suddenly fills the room.

We both look toward Miles, who sets his phone playing music on the table in front of him.

"There's plenty of room to dance here," he says.

"According to Michael?" Brooke taunts.

"According to me."

Brooke starts toward the door, but a hand shoots out to pull her back. Miles pulls her toward him in a move as smooth as one he'd pull on the basketball court. She collides with his chest.

"I'll prove it." His voice is pure confidence as his arms wrap around her.

I bite my cheek and pretend to focus on my work, but out of the corner of my eye, I watch them turn on the dance floor.

Where's the popcorn when you need it?

"I'm so sorry. I was pulled away." The wedding planner returns with her iPad in hand, an apologetic smile on her face.

"What were you saying about the configuration not having enough room to dance?" the planner goes on.

Brooke jumps away from Miles, pressing a hand to her neck as if she's warm there.

"I guess we can make it work."

NOVA

Two days until the wedding

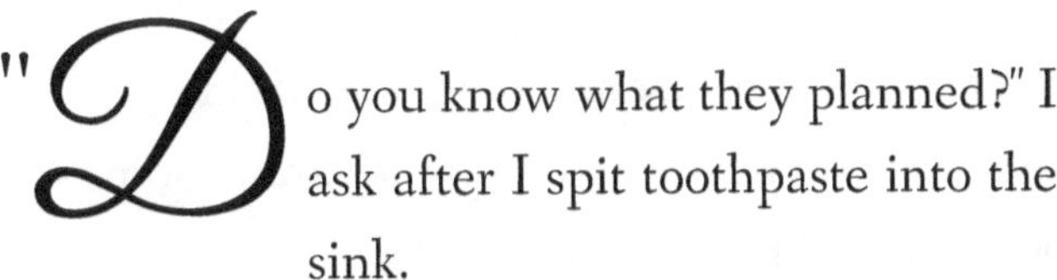

"Do you know what they planned?" I ask after I spit toothpaste into the sink.

Clay towels off his hair behind me. "Not a clue. Tried to beat it out of Rookie on the court, but he's gotten tougher over the last year."

It's the morning of the bachelor and bachelorette parties, and we're getting ready for the day. My fiancé looks handsome as ever with his dark tattoos curling around his arms and chest. He fills the doorway of our ensuite bathroom, a towel wrapped around his hips.

My attention roams over every inch of his hard body. All I can think of is how good he feels against me. How in another couple of weeks, I'll be without him for days and sometimes weeks on end.

Clay steps closer, his gaze drifting down my face to my lips as though he's thinking the same thing. "You wanted to ask me something?"

Since Miles hinted that Clay is working on a secret project, I haven't found the right moment to ask him.

There's a huge list of things to do today—starting with practice for him—but I can't seem to move my feet. Or any other part of me.

"Do you have any regrets we aren't going to go to Paris?" I ask.

When we talked about eloping, we'd tossed around all kinds of places. Paris was top on our list because I love the art, and Clay would too, given all his tattoos. The street art and graffiti alone are incredible.

"I'll take you anytime you like."

Except during the season, he means, which is bearing down on us.

"I wanted to show it to you. You show me so many things that it would be like returning the favor."

"You owe me nothing, Nova. You breathe and I'm grateful. Understand?"

I'm wearing pajamas, and the intensity of his expression makes me suddenly aware of the space between us. My nipples harden under the fabric, the tug between my thighs making me press my legs together. I inhale sharply as he bends closer, the space between us disappearing an inch at a time.

Clay whispers, "You've got toothpaste. Here." His thumb brushes the corner of my mouth.

"Dammit." I spin and rinse my mouth.

When I straighten, he's pinning my hips against the vanity. "You're cute like that."

"With toothpaste sticking to my face?" I ask wryly.

"Like everything."

My heart skips as my eyes meet his in the mirror.

This is what I want. Time with him.

"Clay, can we please—"

A ringtone explodes from the next room.

"It's my parents." I want to tell him to ignore it, but he answers. "Hi." Listens for a minute, then passes over the phone. "It's for you."

I frown as I take the phone from him.

His mother's voice streams out on speaker. "Nova, I wondered if we could meet today."

She's making an effort.

My mind is telling me to say no, but with Clay's eyes on me, I want to at least try.

"I have a dress fitting, but..."

"I'll join you."

That's how, an hour later, I'm on a sofa in the boutique, waiting for them to bring out my dress. My knees press together, my hands twisting. I'm not so much nervous about the dress as the woman at my side. Today she's dressed in a navy pantsuit as if she's about to walk into a board meeting.

"Clay said he has practice this morning," Sandy says while we wait.

I nod, smoothing down my sweaterdress. "Even a wedding can't stop the preseason."

She sits daintily at my side, one ankle crossed over the other. "My dress was a cream sheath dress." Her eyes shine as she remembers.

"I could barely sit in it because... well, let's just say the fabric was unforgiving."

"I bet it was beautiful."

Her lips soften.

I want Clay's parents to like me, but especially Sandy. Not only because my mom isn't here anymore and I want someone to smile at me with approval and admiration when I walk down the aisle, but because we both have a relationship with Clay and we both love him.

"Did you have a bachelorette party?" I ask.

"We didn't. Everything about our wedding moved quickly."

It's clear from her tone that quickly is equivalent to bad.

"I understand our wedding might seem to have come out of nowhere," I start, "but sometimes life moves fast and it feels as if we're barely keeping up. That doesn't diminish how much we care about each other. And we're both so happy that you came."

She tilts her head. "Clayton is our only son. He means the world to us."

The sincerity in her voice feels like an olive branch. I grab onto it.

"He means the world to me, too."

A moment passes between us where I feel as if we have a connection. It starts a spark of hope deep in my chest.

With a tiny nod, she rises from the chaise and wanders toward one of the racks of gowns. The boutique is filled with whites of every shade: cream and beige, Chantilly and ecru. From the carpet to the walls to the gowns, everything is clean and soft.

"Brides overdo it with these layered monstrosities," she says, stroking a layer of taffeta. Her words are quiet, as if she's confiding in me and doesn't want the store associate to hear. "They look like cake toppers, don't you think?"

"Thank you for your patience!" the store attendant calls as a huge garment bag is marched out from the back.

She and another attendant work together to unzip the bag and pull out the gown. My breath catches again as I take in the fitted top, the delicate lace appliques covering the bodice, and the skinny straps that tie over my shoulders. The way the waist explodes into layers of tulle.

I go behind the curtain to undress, and they help me into the gown.

The first thing I notice is how it feels. It's soft and lush, every inch clinging to my body. It's light and airy, but when I step out from behind the curtain and onto the dais, the skirt swishes around me. I love how I look.

"What do you think?" one of the attendants asks, but she's already smiling.

"It's beautiful," I murmur as I turn, admiring it from the side. Peering over my shoulder, I glimpse the low-cut back.

I feel like a princess.

No, a queen.

"Mother of the bride, what do you think?"

"Mother of the groom," Sandy corrects as she turns and does a double-take.

Her expression twists in a few different directions before she commits to one.

She hates it. Her lips are pressed together as if it takes everything in her to not say the words.

"What are you doing with your hair?" she asks finally.

"I was thinking of wearing it half up and half down."

"I meant the color. You're not planning to walk down the aisle with pink hair!"

Sandy says it as if she's stating what's perfectly obvious to any rational person. But when I don't respond, her laughter dies.

The comment about my hair is what puts me over the edge.

I press my hands to my face. *This is exactly why people elope.*

"Excuse me?"

I open my eyes to find her staring in shock.

Her shock becomes mine when I realize I said it out loud.

There's no taking it back. No playing it off as a joke.

I swallow. "We were going to elope. With all the complications..." I trail off.

Maybe we should have.

It's clear from her expression that she's finished my sentence in her head.

She spins on a kitten heel and stalks out the door, letting it bang against the frame on the way out. She disappears around the corner before I drop onto the couch and blink back tears.

Guilt and defeat collide in my chest. I've

been trying so hard to forge a relationship with Clay's mom, but somehow, I've made everything worse.

I could call him, but he's busy with his own priorities.

My phone buzzes with a text.

Brooke: Hey, Miss Bride. Are you ready for a night you'll never forget?! Or maybe one you won't remember...

I text back, my fingers flying over the keypad.

Nova: Does that mean there will be alcohol?

Brooke: More than you could dream of.

I exhale hard.

Nova: Then yes I am.

∼

"No peeking!" Mari says.

"That's easy because you blindfolded me," I point out, the black satin fabric obscuring any hint of light or where we are.

"And no phones. No contact with the outside world." Brooke plucks the phone from my fingers. "You said the dress fitting went fine, so there's no reason you need to be on the phone."

"The dress looks great," I say.

"But...?"

"But Clay's mom hated it, and I said something that upset her." I fold my arms and turn toward the window even though I can't see outside.

The frustrations from earlier piled up right until my friend knocked on my door to ambush me.

"Evil mothers-in-law are a rite of passage," Brooke had declared. "Tonight, you can forget all of it. No parents. No cameras. Just the girls."

"Where exactly are we going?" I ask for the fifth time as I stick my head toward the front seat. "And why did you tell me to wear a sports bra?"

They don't answer until we pull up. They

help me out of the car and up a set of stairs. The hushed voices outside give way to familiar ones.

"Kat, is that you?" I call, waving my hands in the air.

"I'm here," she responds, sounding amused.

"Who else?"

"Chloe."

They let me pull off my bandana, and I spin around the room. "Wait, we're in a strip club?"

The space is full of pulsing lights. A low bass track throbs through hidden speakers. Plus, a raised stage takes up half the room. But instead of a single pole in the center of the stage, there are six poles evenly spaced out.

The girls are standing around wearing various forms of athletic wear. From Mari's sleek black outfit to Brooke's gold cropped top and shorts to Kat's yoga pants and tank and Chloe's leopard-print outfit.

"We're doing a pole class to get you moves-ready, wifey," Brooke announces.

Excitement washes away any bad feelings from earlier. I love dancing, and the idea of shaking away my frustrations is immensely appealing. Still, the poles are slick and silver, and all I can picture is J.Lo doing upside-down splits halfway up one through some magical core strength that's not available to us mortals.

"I warned you—Nova's not coordinated." Mari laughs.

"I move to my own rhythm," I counter.

My sister puts her hands on her hips. "What about the time you tripped racing on flat pavement when you were ten?"

"For the thousandth time, there was something lying across the road."

"Transparent aliens? Invisible roadkill?" Mari says helpfully.

"Let's do it," I decide. I need to unleash my energy on something. I love the idea of swinging around the pole in elegant circles, even if I have no idea how I'd get there. "But can I have a drink first?"

The girls cheer and it's settled.

A bartender brings us margaritas—or "Bridearitas" as he calls them—and we toast. I take a long gulp of one before setting the rest on the coffee table in front of a chaise longue facing the stage.

The instructor comes over and introduces

herself as Anna. Her blond hair is pulled back in a stubby ponytail, and her strong, toned legs are clad in yoga shorts. "Over the next ninety minutes, we're going to have fun and get a hell of a workout, and on top of that, there's a prize for whoever does the best routine at the end."

Brooke hollers, clapping.

"I love a prize," Kat declares.

"But first, you need the proper uniforms." Anna grabs a basket full of feather boas from the corner and passes them out to us.

"Don't strangle yourself," Chloe warns.

"They'll break if you put weight on them," Anna assures us.

Our instructor starts us off by moving around the pole, hooking an arm around it, and going into a back bend.

"I'm too old for this," Mari complains, her hair brushing the floor.

"Maybe you're just too married," Chloe teases. "Your motivation decreased. Harlan's head over heels and divorce is expensive."

My sister throws a boa at Chloe, which flutters to the floor halfway to its target.

"Good job, ladies. It's getting harder." Anna

goes to crank up the music, the bass getting under my skin until I feel as if I'm part of it.

My sister taps out, going for her margarita.

"What, you're done?" I complain.

She drops onto the couch facing the poles with a sigh of satisfaction. "I'm rehydrating. I got three hours with my eyes closed last night. Sleep regression is a real thing." She takes a long sip of her drink and motions to Chloe, who finishes her move and joins Mar.

The rest of us throw ourselves into moves of increasing difficulty. There's no J.Lo inverted split, although Brooke gets impressively close.

I catcall at her. "Has Miles seen those moves?"

She tries to flip me off but can't from her position.

"Who's Miles?" Kat asks, grinning.

"He's on the Kodiaks," I say, enjoying my role as instigator for a change. "Plays with Clay. And Brooke's brother, Jay."

"Wait, your brother's on the team?" Kat asks.

Brooke nods.

"And you're into this guy Miles?"

"No."

I grab my drink and take a gulp. "Didn't look like that in the reception room."

This time Brooke does flip me off.

The rest of the time flies by. The dancing is incredibly challenging, but it feels good at the same time. Things are simple when it's just you and a metal bar.

Simpler still with one margarita down and a second replacing the empty glass immediately.

"Who's ready for the dance-off?" Anna asks when we've stopped for a break and to chug a bunch of water. "It's your own original choreography, and you get to pick the song. You have five minutes to prepare."

When it's time to go, Kat starts. She chooses Bloodhound Gang, and we scream our approval. She's strong and athletic, and even though she and Clay look different, it seems the athletic gene runs in the family.

Then it's Brooke, and she does even better.

Then it's my turn, and I do my routine to Backstreet Boys.

I start with some simple struts, gearing up for a big finish where I swing around the pole.

By the end, the screaming is out of control.

"Nova is the winner!" Anna declares, and I lift my hands and my boa in the air.

The bartender tops up our drinks, and Brooke brings out a package. "This is for you."

Winning has its perks. I dig through the tissue paper, but there's not much there. Finally, my fingers close around what feels like lace. I pull my hand out to hold up the world's tiniest G-string.

"It was a special order," Brooke says.

"Of what, dental floss?"

Mari gasps, Chloe snorts along with Kat, and Brooke grins with pride. I turn it over and see the scrap of lace has something embroidered on it.

Clay's jersey number.

"There's a bra too."

I go fish for that one, pulling up barely more floss than before. One boob says "Mrs." and the other says "Wade."

"It's your 'yes, ma'am' outfit. Every girl has to have one. The one that makes a guy say yes to anything she wants."

"This contest was clearly rigged," I decide.

"Never," Brooke says, mock offended.

It feels good to be here with my friends,

feeling accepted and loved and excited for this wedding.

"Is it weird talking about your brother like this?" I ask Kat after I set the gift on top of a pile of our belongings on the table.

"Totally. But I'm glad it's you." She squeezes my hand.

Her words mean the world to me, but they also remind me Kat grew up with Clay's parents too.

"I'm not sure your mom likes me."

"Ah, Nova." Kat snorts, her eyes kind. "Welcome to the family. She hates everyone."

"She doesn't hate Clay." I honestly can't understand why a person would be so judgmental all the time.

She sighs. "It's complicated, but I will tell you that she was pregnant with Clay when she got married. I'm not sure she would have picked my dad if it wasn't for the circumstances. They were never wildly in love or anything like that, but they've always been able to come together around a cause. Clay was their original cause, and the fact that he's their greatest one is some reminder that she made the right choice."

My chest squeezes as compassion edges in. I guess I can understand why she's cautioning us from making a quick decision.

"What are you doing?" Brooke demands from behind me.

"It's a gag gift. You can't think she's ever actually *wearing* it," my sister scoffs.

"How the hell do you know that?"

My mouth falls open as I spot Mari holding the bottom of my gift over a trash bin in the corner while Brooke tries to wrestle my sister away from it with the top.

"YOU GUYS!" I holler.

They freeze. It would be comical if it wasn't for the intensity on their faces.

I cross to them, aware of Kat and Chloe behind us but beyond caring.

We're all friends, or we're supposed to be.

"I don't know what's happening this week, but I love you both." My attention turns on my sibling, her face flushed. "Mari, no one will ever replace you as my one and only sister." I turn to take in my friend, who's breathing heavily, the triangle top still clutched in her grip. "Brooke, you're the friend I always needed and I'm so grateful you came into my life."

They look at each other guiltily.

"I just wanted everything to be perfect," Mari says to me.

"You deserve an amazing wedding," Brooke adds.

"The biggest reason I wanted to do the wedding here is so I could share it with both of you," I insist. "So stop fighting because I hate shouting at two of my favorite people."

I wrap an arm around each of them and drag them close for a group hug.

"I was just getting rid of something you'd never wear," Mari mumbles against my shoulder.

"I know." I work the bottoms out of her hand and pass them behind my back to Brooke.

"I'll put these in your bag," she whispers when my sister steps back. I give her a thumbs up.

Sudden music has all of us looking up.

"Time for your real prize!" calls the bartender. He strips off the top of his suit and climbs up on stage.

I grab Brooke's hand, the other flying to my face as I gasp. Shrieks go up, replaced with appreciative hollers as he dances. We watch and laugh and dance ourselves.

"I wonder what the guys are doing," Chloe calls over the music.

Brooke's expression turns smug as though she's sitting on a goldmine of info. "How badly do you want to know?"

13

CLAY

"What is this place?" Atlas grunts.

"Welcome to the Garden of the Gods." Miles grins as he gets out of the limo.

The massive park is filled with rock formations the color of pottery ascending toward the sky.

I stare up at the huge red rock jutting overheard.

Jay follows my gaze. "Seems pretty tall. Not sure our contracts cover climbing."

"It's nothing," Atlas says.

"Speak for yourself." Rookie grins. Atlas has four inches on any of us.

"Only thing your pretty head needs to

worry about right now is the Champions Challenge," says Miles with a flourish. "It's like an escape room, but we're outdoors. The prize is this." He opens a case next to him.

It's the championship trophy.

"How the hell did you get your hands on that?"

The team has had it for the past few months, but it's supposed to be housed in a safe location. This—a national park with zero guards and a few hundred tourists and infinite places to bury it—hardly seems right.

"Call it a favor. A wedding gift for our fearless leader." He nods toward me. "Winner gets to keep it for an entire month. Use it for whatever you like."

"So, a doorstop?" Jay drawls. "It's not even a cup. You can't eat cereal out of it."

Miles frowns. "It's the damned trophy, man. Show some respect."

He explains the rules and we break into teams.

"What happens to the losing team?" I drawl.

"Losing team has to take a naked ice bath."

"That's it?"

"In front of everyone," he decides.

All the guys cringe.

We do our share of icing for physical therapy, but doing it when you're not hurting sucks.

Not that I know where we're getting an ice bath around here anyway.

We start with a scavenger hunt where we have to track down random items: a certain plant, a bird, something with a Kodiaks logo that none of us brought.

Rookie and I team up. Figure he's young and has good knees.

At one point, we cross paths with Miles, who's eating popcorn. "Something salty," he says through a mouthful.

My intuition about my teammate pays off when there's a climbing race at the end.

Rookie and I win. He leaps into the air, getting high enough that I wonder why he doesn't get more dunks in games.

"How are we supposed to split this?" Rookie asks, nodding to the trophy.

A half dozen tourists pass us, one whispering to another and pointing in our direction.

"There's a camp ground reserved for us." Miles points down one of the dirt paths.

"We the only ones staying there?" Jay asks once they've passed.

"Nah, it's public, but there won't be a problem. I booked us two campsites together." Miles says that as if it's going to make a difference.

Maybe he's right. Could be I'm worn out from what we've been dealing with in terms of public pressure and interest, and we can have a quiet night just the guys, staring up at the stars.

The sound of a muted shriek has me turning to find a half dozen women, one dressed in white with a sash across her chest.

"Ohmigod, it's the Kodiaks!" she gasps, grabbing her friend's arm.

It's a bachelorette. Go figure.

"Where you guys from?" Rookie asks before I can get us out of there.

"Vegas," they chorus.

"Can we take pictures?" the bride begs.

"Come on, Clay. They came all the way from Vegas," Miles insists.

"Just one," I concede.

We pose with the girls. One turns into

three turns into more, and a crowd is starting to gather.

"Man, we're bigger than Taylor Swift right now," Miles crows as we finish.

One of the girls bounces on her heels. "Guys, I just posted this to social and it's blowing up!"

Shit.

My phone rings, and the call display makes my brows rise.

"Yeah?" I grunt.

"Clay, it's the mayor. I hope you don't mind that I got your number from James." My hand tightens on the handset, but she keeps going before I can respond. "One of my staff tipped me off that you're at the Garden of the Gods. Will you be there for another hour? I can have a camera crew there shortly."

"No cameras," I grit out.

"But you're at a Colorado landmark! It's the perfect photo op."

"I said I'd promote the region, and I will. Just not two days before my wedding." I click off and turn back to the guys.

"Everything good?" Jay asks.

"Yeah, fine. But we can't stick around here,"

I say, glancing toward the road. "If we're lucky, we've got ten minutes before every tourist in the park finds us."

It's worse.

Five minutes later, the park descends into chaos.

Crowds of people everywhere pour into the landscape.

When we're on team business, there's security with us, but this was just supposed to be low key.

A group of short fans in purple swarm us. Kids, I realize.

"Guys, no pics today—" I say as I scan the horizon to look for an exit route, but they interrupt.

"We don't want pics. We're here to rescue you."

"That was insane," Miles calls as he steps off the school bus, hi-fiving Rookie as we follow the campers into the dining hall at Kodiak Camp.

I get what he means. The adrenaline

pumping through my veins is usually reserved for game day.

Turns out the kids who found us were wearing not only Kodiaks colors but Kodiaks Foundation Camp shirts. I don't know any of them by name, but more than one face is familiar from the time I've spent at the camp over the years.

They smuggled us out to their bus and convinced the driver to take us back with them, helping avoid the shitstorm that would've happened in a few more minutes.

The staff make room for us at dinner, then invite us to join the campers around the evening's bonfire.

It's not what we planned. It's better.

The vibe is charged but it's a different energy. These kids don't want a piece of us, they want to be us.

The campers jump in with questions. "What's it like to play pro?"

"Hard," I admit. "It's the hardest thing in the world."

"And the best one," Miles weighs in.

"But now that you've won, it gets easier?"

Jay's the first to answer. "Seeing how amped

everyone is around here... we appreciate it, but it adds to the pressure."

"You have lots of money. And fame. You can do anything you want."

"Not everyone's in the same position," I point out. "Some guys off the bench need every contract negotiation, every season, every game to make it work."

"But you don't."

I think of Nova. "I've got people I want to impress. That never goes away."

They're quiet a minute, processing.

"But the winning is fucking great," one kid adds with a laugh.

"Yeah. It's pretty fucking great," I admit.

We hang out with the kids for a while, then the counselors force them off to bed. When it's just us left around the fire, we fall silent. The flames crackle, heat licking the wood until it snaps and pops.

"You ever go to camp here?" Rookie asks, looking around. "Seems like a cool place."

"Not here, but a place like it," I say. "Best part was sneaking food out of the kitchen... and swimming."

"What's that sound?" Jay demands, and they all look around.

"It's my stomach. Come on," I say.

We break into the kitchen for midnight snacks, then roast the marshmallows we found over the fire. We cackle like little kids.

"Two days until game day," Jay notes.

"The wedding?" My lips twitch at his description.

"Forget the season, this is a big deal. You'll be the first one married," Atlas says to me. "You're going to have kids and forget all about us."

"It'll never happen," I say firmly.

"Things will be different this year. Not only with you being married, but the team coming off the championship," Miles says.

The other guys shift as we all process that.

"James wants us to be bigger," Jay says. "We're not only doing this for us and Denver— we're doing it for everyone in Colorado. Every person who's been part of this organization."

"This is our home now," I say. "It's an honor, if you think about it."

This place has been good for me, good to me. The city, the team. My life has had its ups and downs, but I've got a woman I can't live without, a team of guys who make magic together, and the support of an entire state.

A text comes in from my realtor.

Just confirming that you're passing on the house from yesterday. They're taking offers today, and I know it checked most of your boxes.

Yeah, but it wasn't right.

Bitter defeat chases through me.

I wanted to do this for Nova, and now I'm going to let her down.

"Losing teams have got to swim in the cold lake." Jay interrupts my thoughts.

Miles hollers. "Naked!"

We take off toward the lake. Rookie and I might've won, but it's no fun standing alone on the shore.

I strip off my shirt and toss it to the side. Ahead of me, Miles is already working on his shorts.

"Toughen up," Miles calls over his shoulder.

What the hell.

I strip everything off, and the other guys do

too. We splash into the water, Rookie hollering at the frigid temperature.

"You'll wake the campers," I grunt.

"They're kids. They run on candy and basketball, same as you and me did," Miles tosses back.

"Some of us still do. That's right, I saw you sneak PopTarts from the kitchen." Rookie smirks.

Miles dunks him.

My lips twitch despite myself.

For a moment, we're kids again. It's the best feeling. I forget sometimes that we don't have to be grownups. That the goals we set for ourselves are made up, and sometimes, joy comes from living in the moment.

A sound in the bushes near shore draws my gaze, and I swear I see a light glint twice. But the longer I look, the more I decide I made it up.

"Well, well, what have we here?"

Miles' attention snaps up over my shoulder, and I turn to see what, or rather who, is on shore.

The girls are standing on the sand. Nova

and Brooke are in the middle, plus Mari. Kat's on one side, Chloe on the other.

But it's Brooke who has a beach bag dangling from one hand.

"What's in the bag?" Miles usually sounds assured, but there's a wary edge to his voice now.

Brooke plants a hand on her hip. "Wouldn't you like to know."

Could be my camper intuition, but something feels off, even before the first drop of rain hits my face.

Groans go up as the others feel it too. The drops fall faster, cold against my skin.

Jay starts toward the beach, then pulls up. "Guys. Where the fuck are our clothes?"

In Brooke's bag.

I don't care about walking around naked—the guys have seen everything in the changing room. But I'd rather not do it at camp with kids and staff running around.

"Don't do anything stupid," Kat warns, shielding her eyes with a hand.

In a flurry of laughter, they're gone.

14

NOVA

The sand slips under my feet as I run up the hill. We all head for the car, nerves and excitement twining together in a bundle of pulsing energy.

"Think they can find other clothes?" Mari pants.

"They will. But I don't only have their clothes..." Brooke grins.

"My phone is in there!" Miles hollers after us.

They're chasing us, and closing in by the sounds of it.

My lungs burn from the effort. I need to work out more.

The moon shines overhead as I bolt for one

of the cabins that doesn't have campers' gear outside the front door.

It's empty, but it's also dark. I don't want to hit the lights, so I take a few steps inside. The girls follow me in.

"Quick, hide!" I whisper.

Brooke ducks behind the headboard of the bottom bunk. I slip into the closet. Chloe squats behind a dresser. Where the other girls went is beyond me, but Brooke's the one who matters, with her bag of clothes.

My heart hammers against my ribs.

"They didn't see us," Brooke whispers loudly.

Chloe shushes her.

The door creaks open, and every muscle in me tightens. It's like a horror movie. I can't see who's in the doorway as it swings wide. A single footstep makes the boards groan, then another. The huge figure, a dark silhouette, appears around the door.

"Who's there?" it asks.

Clay.

"Out the window," Brooke whispers.

I yank the closet door open and lunge across the floor. Clay's moving the same way.

The girls make it out. I'm reaching for the sill when a hand grabs my ankle and tugs me against a hard body.

"You're in trouble," he purrs in my ear.

I twist to look back over my shoulder, taking in the T-shirt with the Kodiak Foundation logo illuminated by the shaft of moonlight from the window. It's stretched across a thick chest and bulging biceps.

"Seems like skinny dipping in the lake after dark should land you in trouble too," I toss breathlessly.

I reach a hand back, brushing a pair of shorts that are too tight. A giggle rises up before I can stop it.

He spins me, the hard ledge of the window pressing against my shoulders. "Give me back my clothes and maybe I'll let you off easy."

"Brooke has them."

"Which means…"

"You're stuck in those clothes," I say at the same time he says, "We're alone in this cabin."

The thrill of being chased, of chasing, gives way to a different desire.

The weight of the past few days has piled

up. Seeing him like this, playful and competitive, is sexy as hell.

"What'd you get up to tonight?" he murmurs.

"Pole dancing."

He angles his head. "Definitely going to need a repeat performance of that."

Brooke forgot to tell me to bring a change of clothes to the event, so I changed into my underwear "gift" from her to freshen up. Now the thin fabric, if you can call it that, rubs my breasts and between my thighs.

"What about you?" I ask, my voice lower than usual.

"We ran into another bachelorette. They were fans of ours."

I pull back an inch. "Kodashians."

"You're pretty when you're jealous."

"Why would I be jealous? Your dick's in my hand." When I drop my gaze, I appreciate again what he's wearing. A laugh slips out.

The sound of rain outside intensifies, drowning out everything except the odd shriek.

We're not really alone in this place.

Technically we're still on our bachelor and bachelorette parties.

All of which seems way less important than the way Clay's looking at me.

"I missed you," I blurt. "I know you're busy with everything, but I was hoping we'd get to spend this time together."

Clay bends his face to mine. "Me too. I've been working on something..."

"It's okay. The season is about to start—"

"I've been trying to buy us a house. A place for us to build a life together. I wanted it done before we got married, because it was supposed to be a wedding present for you." He exhales hard.

I shift back an inch to take him in. "A house," I echo.

Clay nods. "One that's got everything you could wish for, where you feel like you're at home whether you've had the best day or a terrible one. Being with you is a damned dream come true. I want all your dreams to come true too."

My heart skips.

Of the things I expected him to say, that wasn't it.

"I've been trying to find the right place. Looked at dozens, but nothing was good enough," he goes on, and the stubborn edge of his voice makes my lips twitch. "Nothing was close enough to your family, or had the perfect room for you to do your paintings, or had a room with a view where we could watch the sun hovering over the mountains and think about the first time I took you to Red Rocks."

He's always accepted the realities of life on the road, the trade-offs of being a basketball star. Hearing that he's been committed to putting down roots here with me, realizing how much effort he put into this makes me swoon.

"I know you hate finding out you can't do everything yourself on your terms, but it's kind of endearing," I murmur.

"Oh yeah?" He cocks his head.

"Mhmm."

My ribs ache as I cup his face. "We'll find the perfect house together. And as for feeling like home..." My lips brush across his. "You've always been my home, Clay. Since before I knew I was missing one."

He rests his forehead against mine, throat working. "You're it for me, Pink. I would trade everything I've done in this life for a single day as your husband."

He's kissing me now, with the kind of lazy possession that makes my knees weak.

I love him, and I want him. There's nothing like being alone with this man. No matter how complicated the world is outside, he's everything I need.

He reaches under my top, his hand brushing the mesh of my bra. "What is this?"

"A gift from Brooke."

I lift my shirt and he takes me in, exhaling hard. His hands sit on my hips, refusing to budge as I work the leggings down.

A mirror in the corner shows me a glimpse of us. The fabric covers exactly nothing—my nipples and a tiny patch between my thighs.

A bolt of lightning illuminates the cabin, and Clay takes in the number. His name. His brows rise under the damp fall of his hair.

"You're so fucking sexy. If you knew how weak you make me."

I love the way he wants me. It's like being caught in a raging fire, burning up until I'm part of the same flames consuming me.

His breath fans my face as he pulls back an inch. "The guys'll find somewhere to crash until the rain is over." Clay's fingers thread into my hair, angling my face. "You, on the other hand, won't be going anywhere."

"That doesn't sound like something a good man would say to his fiancée," I tease.

"No. It's something a desperate man would say to his wife."

He throws me over his shoulder, and I shriek as he tosses me on the top bunk and follows me up. He bends over me, pressing his lips lightly to my collarbone. His kisses fall across my skin, each one startlingly gentle.

His hair is damp from the lake, and mine is from the rain.

I shiver, and he wraps a blanket around us, then starts down my body.

"*Mrs. Wade.*"

"Brooke's idea," I murmur.

"Remind me to thank her for that." His lips skip across my breast. Then close on the peak through the fabric.

The sensation is exquisite. Pleasure tightens through me, a velvet rope pulling tight. He's a puppet master with that mouth, those hands, and I'm dancing on his strings.

"I love seeing my name on you. Knowing it's going to be your name too." His touch skims down between my thighs where his number rests. It's blatant possession, a marking of his territory.

He brushes along the edge of the scrap of fabric, rubbing the string along my wet slit.

Clay presses where I'm soaked. He sinks inside, filling me with first one thick digit then two. "Ride my fingers."

I couldn't say no if I tried. My body needs him, and the way he's looking at me, not with possession but total adoration, I can't deny him anything.

"That's it, Pink," he murmurs against my ear, brushing the hair from my damp face. "You're so beautiful. Best fucking part of my life."

My chest expands with longing, and love.

"Ditto," I whisper, my hand cupping his face.

He turns his lips in toward my palm, and I arch against his fingers.

"I need you," I murmur.

He doesn't strip the thong off or rip it. Instead, he yanks it to the side.

"Nova," he groans as he sinks in an inch at a time. "So fucking good. So fucking *mine*."

Clay makes me feel as if my heart could beat out of my chest. As if I could float away with pleasure. It also feels as if I'm taking my life into my hands because he's so huge and male and determined, and I wonder if I might split open at any second.

It'd be worth it.

My nails rake down his back.

He groans, thrusting harder.

The bunk bed creaks under the weight of our movement.

He's a god. Big and dark and brutal.

I'm his weakness. Bright and soft and sweet like candy.

And I'm getting closer. Every stroke of his hips that hits me in just the right place drags me toward the edge. His fingers dig into my ass as I arch to meet him. His lips brush my temple. My arms band around his back, holding him close.

Then I can't take it anymore.

"That's it, Pink. Come all over me."

Soon he's shaking too.

I whisper his name and tremble as the pleasure consumes me. I'm like kindling in the campfire outside, burned up until there's nothing left but smoke drifting in the air.

After, he's careful not to crush me with his body, shifting us so he's on his side.

It takes at least a minute, maybe ten, before the stars behind my eyes stop.

A shiver runs through me.

"Still cold?" he murmurs, his lips against my bare shoulder.

"No." I shake my head and lift the scrap of fabric that makes up the bra top.

He chuckles and wraps me in his arms until his heartbeat matches mine.

CLAY

The day before the wedding

The sun slices through the window, a lazy beam that matches my energy when I crack an eye open.

Nova's curled against my side. Her hair falls across the pillow in a wave. I can't resist brushing a hand through it, and she stirs.

"Morning," I murmur.

"Morning." Her sleepy smile is brighter than the damned sun.

My legs tangle with hers, the sheets twisted

around us both. My feet extend past the end of the mattress.

She stretches her hands overhead, yawning. The yawn's replaced with a wince as she shifts onto her side.

"Sore?" I ask.

"A little."

The things I did to make her that way flash through my mind, a sexy slideshow. "I'll be thinking of that on my next road trip."

Her smile fades a little. "I'm excited that you guys have a chance to defend your season. But I'm also sad I won't see you as much."

"Me too." I tuck a piece of hair behind her ear. "Tell you what—after this wedding, let's get out of town for a few days. We'll have a real honeymoon down the road, but for now, we'll get away just the two of us."

She sucks in a breath. "Paris?"

"Fuck, yeah."

It'll be tough to negotiate with the coaching staff, but I'll make it happen. Nova's too close, too naked, too in love with me for me to settle for anything else.

"This whole week has been a bit crazier than I expected," my fiancée admits.

My abs flex. My girl can spot the rainbow in every thunderstorm, and the possibility that she's been hiding the rougher side of things has me instantly on guard.

"You regret deciding to get married here?"

She lifts a bare shoulder. "Brooke and Mari have been great, but also a lot. And I'm still figuring your mom out. I guess I play things direct, and I have to think about what I say before I say it."

The idea of Nova feeling self-conscious or trying to change herself sets my teeth on edge.

"You're my fiancée and you're perfect exactly how you are."

She winces. "Even if I might have let it slip at my dress fitting yesterday that we were thinking of eloping? And made your mom leave?"

Shit. I hate the thought of her having to deal with that alone.

"Even then. But I'm pretty sure you can't 'make' my mom do anything." I brush my mouth over hers. "I wish you had told me sooner."

"I'm sorry—"

"Not because of my mom. Because I would have been there to have your back."

Nova's smile lights up the entire room. "I love you."

"Not as much as I love you." She starts to argue, but I'm already shaking my head. "I'm twice your size, so it's physically impossible."

Her blue eyes dance. The curve of her lips drags my attention down...

"You said you were sore," I murmur. "How sore?"

Those pretty eyes darken as I trace a hand down her side towards her hip.

A pounding on the door makes the entire cabin vibrate. "Clay! You're gonna want to see this."

It's Miles.

So much for time alone.

I shift out of bed and tug on shorts before opening the door. When I pull it wide, they're standing outside in...

"What the hell are you wearing?"

Miles holds out his arms, the sleeves of the hoodie riding up nearly to his elbows. "They didn't have my size."

Jay's clothes almost fit. Behind them, Atlas looks as if he's been stuffed into baby clothes.

"So, no luck finding Brooke," Nova says as she ducks under my arm, tucking in against my chest.

"She wouldn't tell us where she put our clothes. We searched everywhere, including the car."

Jay holds out his phone. "We've got another issue."

Chloe descends, Brooke following her and carrying a bag.

"You guys are in *so* much trouble," Chloe warns.

"At least we have clothes!" Miles says cheerfully.

Chloe holds out her phone in the center of our circle, showing a darkly lit video of us running through the dark.

"You took that?" Brooke laughs, impressed.

Chloe grins. "It's good to have leverage."

I can see the outline of our bodies, plus two asses.

"Wait, who has a tattoo on their ass?" Nova asks, fascinated.

"Someone is carrying the trophy," Brooke points out.

"We couldn't leave it behind," Jay says reasonably.

"Where *is* the trophy?" Chloe asks.

We look at one another.

The trophy somehow landed in the dining hall cold storage between two vats of soup. After the campers helped us recover it, we dragged ourselves to a grueling practice that felt as if Coach knew exactly how little sleep we all got last night.

Now Kat, Daniel, and my parents, plus Nova and I, have a reservation at one of the fancier restaurants in town. Nova called to say she's running late with Brooke and Mari and insisted we order for her.

"Grad school's been great," Kat says as she finishes her glass of wine.

"Daniel, you're on the faculty?" my mom prompts as she pushes a piece of bread around her plate.

"That's right."

"How old are you?" my dad asks Daniel.

"Old enough I had to be his son's nanny in order to get him to date me," Kat supplies sweetly.

Mom reaches for her water, coughing.

Daniel, to his credit, looks as if he's accustomed to my sister's brand of gives-no-fucks.

They're perfect for each other.

We've just ordered for all of us, Nova included, when I spot the missed call from my realtor. The phone must have been on silent since practice. I make my excuses and step outside long enough to play the message.

"Clay, it's me. I found something you might be interested in—"

"We need to talk," my mother cuts in, coming outside behind me.

My hand tightens on the handset as I lower it to my side. "About?"

"It's this wedding, Clayton." Her brows knit together. "I wish you would slow down and think. Protect yourself."

I stare at her.

From what Nova said, they weren't skipping through fields arm in arm this week, but that's a far cry from trying to stop a wedding.

"I've had nothing but time," I say evenly.

"Then why the short notice? The small guest list? You're distracted, and not thinking clearly. I won't watch you make a mistake you'll regret."

"Mom." I'm battling mounting frustration. "I'm not distracted, I have a lot of things going on."

Her arms cross. "Growing up there were late nights, early mornings, travel to tournaments, this camp or that one, but all of it had a purpose. We wanted to help you become the most that you could be. Now you are, and we don't want you to compromise."

My molars grind together. On a court, I can take out my emotions, but it takes everything in me not to dunk on my mother.

"You raised me to go after what I want. For a long time my career was it. I appreciate how much you and dad did for me my entire childhood. But I love Nova, and if you can't see why, then you aren't looking hard enough."

She steps closer, tilting her chin up

stubbornly. "Is that why you were considering eloping? Because you didn't want us involved?"

She's not pissed about the wedding, I realize. Her criticism covers up the fear and rejection she refuses to acknowledge.

It doesn't excuse how she's acting, but it reminds me how Nova wanted everyone to get along this week. Because even when family's complicated, they're still family.

So instead of shutting down or turning away, I take a breath.

"We were thinking of eloping because our lives have been complicated. How I feel about Nova is simple. She's the love of my life. I'm going to be with her no matter what, and we've spent so much of our time together living on other people's terms that we're ready to start living on ours. The reason we're doing the wedding here is that Nova found the perfect place, and we thought we could have everything we wanted: get married before the season and see the people we love at the same time."

I look back at my phone. "If I seem distracted, it's because I'm getting us a house. I've been trying to track one down for months and promised myself I'd get it before we got married."

Her expression softens with surprise. "A house?"

"When we moved to LA, Nova followed, no questions asked. She made a home for us. One built on trust and kindness, both of which she gave me freely even in the times when I couldn't reciprocate the way I should have. She helped me through the hardest time of my life. I want to make her a home here. To show her there's a place for her to be exactly who she is. One where she'll always belong."

"Am I interrupting?" comes a voice at my back.

Mom's gaze shifts past me and I glance over my shoulder toward the sidewalk.

Nova's standing frozen, looking between me and my mom.

NOVA

I'm late for dinner, and I feel terrible about it.

Working through last-minute decisions

with Brooke and Mari has been a lot. They're helpful and caring but constantly trying to one-up each other.

My head is pounding by the time I make it to the restaurant.

Familiar raised voices reach me from around the corner.

Clay's in a heated conversation with his mom. *Damn it.*

This is exactly what I didn't want to happen.

I force my feet to continue because I can't listen to the argument.

Clay and his mom are standing outside on the sidewalk, staring each other down.

I clear my throat. "Am I interrupting?"

They turn to see me, two sets of similar dark eyes wide with surprise.

There's no pretending this fight isn't about me. I heard enough to know that.

"Nova, could I have a word?" Sandy asks quietly.

Clay moves between us. "I don't think—"

"It's okay," I tell him. "I'll be there in a minute."

He drops a kiss on my forehead. "I'll be right over there," he murmurs.

"Is everything all right?" I ask.

"Clayton told me you convinced him to get married here instead of eloping."

It's such a curveball from what I expected that I'm speechless for a moment. "I wouldn't put it that way, but yes."

She looks contrite, humble even as she presses a hand to her lips. "I'm sorry for how I've acted. Things moved quickly when I was married, perhaps too quickly, and I don't want that for him. But I shouldn't put that on you two."

I turn that over. "Well, I know you're proud of Clay on the basketball court, but I hope you're proud of him in every way. He's an incredible person. He's kind, caring, devoted. We've been through a lot together, and I'm grateful for every day I get to spend with him."

Her eyes widen a little. "You're not what I expected for Clayton, but I've never seen him as serious about any person as he is about basketball. I see the way he loves you, and it's more than I could have hoped for." She clears her throat. "Your dress will be very nice. And your hair."

I swallow the laughter that rises up. "Thank you. If you'll excuse me…"

"Of course."

I catch up with Clay in a quiet hallway by the bathrooms. He's pacing, a hand shoved through his hair with a death-grip on his phone with the other.

"Hey," I say.

He's at my side in an instant, inspecting every inch of my face. "Hey. Everything okay?"

"It will be."

He kisses me, and every thought goes out the window.

"You didn't hear us arguing before you got here?" he asks.

"Only the part about how I'm the love of your life." My chest twinges at the memory. "Thank you for standing up for me."

His eyes crinkle as he brushes a thumb down my cheek. "That part wasn't hard. Never will be. I've got your back every damned day, I just wish you'd let me have it sooner."

I nod to the phone still in his hand. "Everything okay with you?"

"Realtor called with some more houses." I tilt my head, expectant. "I told him we'd look at them together once we're back."

My smile threatens to split my face. "Perfect. You ready to get married?"

He lifts his chin, staring down at me with serious eyes.

"Been ready since the moment you stole my seat on the plane."

16

NOVA

The Wedding Day

"You look incredible," Brooke insists when she enters the doorway of the suite at Little Nell where I'm getting ready.

"So do you."

Her cocktail dress is sleeveless and fitted, the pale pink making her bronze skin even richer.

"I wanted to match the bride without matching the bride." She nods to my pink hair.

I turn in front of the floor-length mirror.

The dress fits to perfection, every line skimming my body.

My hair forms soft waves, the front half pinned up away from my face. The pink is freshly done and subtle. The veil, tucked into the hair comb holding the style together, falls down my back like a waterfall. Soft makeup makes my eyes look bluer, and my cheeks are flushed from the reality of what's happening today rather than makeup.

I feel beautiful. Radiant. A little glamorous.

"How does it feel to be getting married in an hour?" Brooke asks.

"Like I'm living someone else's life," I admit. "I grew up in a trailer moving from place to place. I couldn't keep my life together. I didn't know who I was. And now I'm here." I wave at the lush room surrounding us. The furnishings are plush and rich, the ceiling high enough even Atlas couldn't reach it.

My friend comes over to me. "This is your life, Nova. No one else could pull this off."

I can't help grinning. Brooke's smile falls away as she watches me rise and head toward the doorway of the ensuite.

"Whoa, slow up. Be a good Kodiak and wait

for the assist." Brooke comes to get me as I'm trying to pass through the door. She scoops up the bottom of my gown and wraps it in her hands so I can get in. "There. Need to pee?"

"Nope. Just forgot my necklace." I find it in the jewelry box, the silver locket with our pictures in it. "It was my mom's. She gave it to Mari."

Brooke holds up a hand. "One second."

She disappears, and a moment later, Mari's head sticks through the bathroom door. "Brooke said you needed me?" she says, sounding out of breath.

Love and belonging swell in my chest as Mari helps me put on the necklace.

Kat comes and finds us. "Mom wanted you to have this." She holds up a tiny silver and pink comb. "She said you were wearing your hair up and she didn't know if it would match but she wanted to try."

The mountains stand out in relief against the bright fall sky. Rows of chairs contain our guests, everyone dressed beautifully. The basketball players insisted on sitting in the back because of their heights, so now I can see their eyes as they spot me.

Mari's walking me down to my future husband.

Clay's waiting at the end of the aisle.

It shouldn't be possible for any man to look so godlike. His custom tux barely contains his massive shoulders and torso. The sight of him steals my breath, but it's the expression on his face when he sees me that makes my knees weak.

He loves me.

Has loved me for longer than I would have believed possible if he didn't insist it was true.

I make my way down the aisle to him.

As I do, I think of his words to me before we left one another this morning.

"Hope today is everything you wanted."

Now, I can't see the mountains or the ceremony or the guests. I can only see him as I hear my own whispered response.

"It's more."

17

CLAY

When you spend your life becoming a superstar, you get used to eyes on you.

Now, they're all on her.

Our friends and family are all standing and turned to get a look at Nova as she starts down the path covered with petals, her arm hooked in her sister's.

She's not a rainbow—she's the damned sun.

It's not the dress that clings to every curve I know better than my own body. It's not even the way she moves. It's the way her eyes meet mine. How she shines up at me as if everything I thought was my life was only the preview and today is the main feature.

My breath lodges deep in my chest. The knot gets tighter as she moves toward me. After all the chaos of the past couple of weeks, there's nowhere I'd rather be.

Nova stops inches away from me, her sister kissing her cheek. Mari shoots me a look that says, *Don't fuck this up*, before stepping back to her seat in the front row.

In this moment, we want the same thing.

There were times I didn't think I'd make it here. To this point in my life, not only *here*, surrounded by beauty and mountains and people who've made a difference in my world.

The fact that everyone cared this much to come is touching. I knew people needed me on the court, but seeing them show up this way when they don't need to affects me.

At the center of it all is her.

Nova's the one who makes it all worthwhile.

Thanks to her, I can picture spending a few more years in the league.

Just like I can picture the time after it. Holding my girl in our home. Laughing as we chase around kids that have her curious eyes.

The ceremony is a blur. The officiant's

words echo in my head, but all I'm thinking about is how she's mine.

When I slide the ring on her finger, it feels like certainty. It feels like home.

I swear nothing could be better.

I'm wrong.

When she puts hers on me, it's humbling.

It feels as if I'm on my knees, asking her to have me.

"I love you," she whispers.

I can't talk. My throat is so tight I may never swallow again.

Somehow, I manage to get out the words I need to.

"I do."

"I do."

The officiant speaks again, a monotone that has me spacing out again.

Nova's light scent and the way she's practically vibrating and the shine in her eyes.

"It's done," I hear myself say under my breath.

The officiant stops midsentence. "Well, yes, but..."

I grab Nova's face with one hand and bend to meet her.

Her lips part under mine, and her smile and the way she tastes and her little moans are everything I need.

The crowd erupts, and it's every bit as good as winning a championship.

No. As we walk back down the aisle, her fingers securely woven with mine, the ring heavy on my finger...

It's better.

"Picasso," Brooke insists.

"Picasso didn't do flowers," Mari counters.

"Van Gogh?"

"I'll take it."

"They look good," I say, my hand in Nova's as we come up behind them.

Nova beams. "They do, don't they?"

After the ceremony, we went for pictures. I was getting more distracted the longer we did them, especially when the photographer showed us a few.

"What's wrong?" Nova asked.

"Nothing," I lied.

Now, we eat dinner side by side. It feels right with our friends and family around us.

After, I rise.

"Shut up, everyone, Clay's going to make a speech," Miles says.

Laughter goes up, and I wait until it dies down to talk. "Thank you for being here. If you know me, you know speeches aren't my thing. But sometimes you gotta do what feels out of character."

I turn to Nova. "First time I met you was at thirty thousand feet. Screw mile high, we were up in the clouds." Her lips curve, and I feel the answering tug on mine. "I didn't want to like you. I didn't want to love you. You showed me that being an asshole wasn't the only way, or even the best way, to go through life."

Scattered chuckles sound throughout the guests.

I swallow against the tightness in my ribs.

"You showed me how to love a person, and a place. You changed everything. I promise I will try the rest of my life to make you feel the same way. And if I fuck up, anyone in this room can give me hell for it."

"We will!" Brooke hollers.

Nova's brows lift, her lower lip trembling.

She presses her mouth to mine.

The food comes, and our guests resume their conversations in little groups. People from basketball and outside blend together. Tonight, everyone is family.

My mom leans over my dad toward me. "We're happy for you. Both of you. This is beautiful." She nods to the paintings.

My lips curve as I take in my wife.

Before dessert, I feel Nova squeeze my hand. "Something's on your mind. Please tell me you're not already strategizing for the home opener." Her eyes glint with happiness and humor.

"No," I say.

"Then what?"

I lean toward her, my mouth brushing her ear as I exhale. "I can't wait to take you home."

"Really?" Her lips curve. "Haven't we already done everything?"

"Now that you're my wife, we've got to do it all over again."

By eleven, the dancing is in full swing.

A familiar form who didn't get an invitation appears, flanked by aides in suits.

"Don't worry, I'm not staying. I have a business dinner here in town and stopped on the way to say I'm sorry for causing you grief," the mayor says, holding a wrapped gift.

"This place matters to me. I'll continue to help out where I can," I promise.

She smiles and nods, setting the gift with a pile on the other side of the room before heading back to the doors, aides in tow.

Across the room, my wife is acting something out, her arms gesturing in sweeping circles while the guys laugh. I head her way, and the crowd parts for me.

She's telling a story, her gestures getting wilder. I bite my cheek in amusement. My hands land on her waist, and I draw her back against me.

"Excuse us," I say to the group.

She's light under my hands as I turn her in my grasp, adjusting my grip to pull her close. We move to the music.

"But I was just getting to the good part!" she chides lightly as she tips her face up toward me.

I think about the rest of our lives together. Tonight, the next year, the decades it come.
"You're right about that."

EPILOGUE

NOVA

"Call security."

Clay's voice at my back has me spinning toward him.

"What's wrong?" I demand. He appears to be fine, but he's staring at the wall with an expression of confusion.

We're at the Louvre, looking at expressionist paintings.

"It's upside down," he declares. "It has to be. These are feet, and this is a head. Get a guard over here to fix this, stat."

I giggle and tug Clay's arm. "It's abstract. You're more of a concrete guy."

"You calling me a dumb jock?" he grunts, but there's humor beneath it.

His fingers weave with mine, and the feel of his ring against my skin is a thrill I'll never get used to.

If preparing for the wedding was a whirlwind, the seventy-two hours since have been a dream.

There's nowhere like Paris. The Seine. The Eiffel Tower. The galleries.

The Kodiaks went in together to send us on a mini-moon. Not only for the hotel and flights, but getting Clay three days off on the eve of the season. That request was unprecedented, but they managed to swing it for Clay.

Having Clay to myself has been incredible.

He's attentive, focused only on me and ensuring we have the best time together. Each morning when we've woken up, he's nuzzled me awake, asking, "How did my wife sleep?"

Gah. If I thought there'd be no difference after the wedding, I was so wrong, and it has nothing to do with the fact that everything is half mine on paper.

By the time we finish at the gallery, my stomach is growling and the sun is setting. We eat at a tiny restaurant down a small alley with candlelight and delicious food.

"What's wrong?" I ask as I catch Clay staring into space when I return from the bathroom.

"I can't believe we have to go home tomorrow," he admits.

"Unless you want to run away together." Instead of sitting, I stop in front of him.

His hands go to my hips, pulling me into his lap. "You make it sound good, Pink."

My wrists cross behind his head and I smile. "You'd miss basketball. You'd catch one Kodiaks game in the background of some little sports bar and have a problem with the guys playing differently than you would."

"You know me too well." His eyes crinkle at the corners. "Speaking of going home tomorrow, the realtor sent through a new house. It's close enough to Harlan and Mari you can get there for dinner, but not so close they'd overhear us cursing them."

"You must mean you cursing your GM, because I'd never curse my sister," I say, deadpan.

"Of course not," he replies, equally serious. "It's on two acres of property. Six bedrooms."

"In case we have guests?"

"I was going to say kids. But guests work, too." His grin makes my heart skip. "But the best part is this solarium with floor to ceiling windows and mountain views. You could fill it up with art."

I feel my heart speed up. "It sounds amazing."

"Good. I told him we'd like to see it together."

I kiss him, long and slow. "You're the best."

"Thought I was third best," he grumbles.

"Nope. I was wrong." I grin as I pull back enough to watch stylish people wander by on the street. "It's our final night here. We should spend it in a memorable way."

He looks down at his finger. "I can't wear a ring during the games. I want to get this tattooed on me."

My lips press together. "I have an idea."

After we finish eating, we stroll hand in hand back toward our hotel and stop in front of a tattoo parlor.

Clay gets his wedding ring tattooed on his finger. It's black ink, tiny dots made to look like shading.

"There. I feel better knowing you won't lose

a finger on my account. Or miss a three," I add with a smile. I take a moment to admire the artist's work.

"Now you'll be with me on and off the court."

I drop into the chair. "My turn."

His brows shoot up. "Really?"

"The first time we met, you said you owed me a tattoo. This one's on you."

Clay cocks his head. "I take that to mean you've decided what you want?"

I nod to the artist. "You've got the sketch I sent?"

Realization dawns on Clay's face. "You set this up. You played me."

I wink. "You aren't the only one who's been working on a secret project the last few months."

One of the reasons my commissions have taken a backseat is that I've been working on a single design I wanted to be perfect.

The tattoo Clay promised to get me.

I wanted it to represent us, and I went through dozens of sketches and paintings to get it exactly right.

We didn't land in this tattoo parlor by chance. I did my research and found this incredible artist. She normally books out a year in advance, but when I told her our story, she agreed to make room.

"This might sting a little," she warns as she prepares to work, cleaning the wrist I extend.

Clay holds my other hand.

The tattoo needle buzzes across my skin.

"Does it hurt?"

My lips twitch. "You've had a hundred tattoos, and you're worried about me getting one. You think I'm that fragile?"

"No way." He shakes his head. "Just hate to see you in pain."

It's worth every second when I look down my arm to see the two tiny ranunculus flowers, one purple and one pink, their stems twined together.

After we're finished at the tattoo shop, we walk across the bridge hand in hand. There's street music playing somewhere in the distance, and I swear this is the most romantic place on earth.

"Two truths and a lie," I blurt. "I'll start. I

have a life beyond anything I dreamed. I've never been so happy. And... I'm married to the best basketball player in the world."

"Those all sound true."

I flip my palms, grinning. "I guess they are."

His eyes dance across my face.

"We're really bad at this game," I whisper as his lips claim mine.

This entire week feels surreal. After the most beautiful wedding ceremony celebrating with the people we love most, we flew first class to Paris to celebrate the occasion in a whole new way.

Clay's parents sent us a generous gift. He took me shopping, we went to galleries, and we ate delicious food.

This morning, my hot-as-hell husband woke me up with his tongue between my thighs.

Life is good.

A cell phone vibrates.

"Told them to leave me alone," he says, going to switch it off.

"It's me." I grab for it and see the guys are calling on FaceTime. I laugh, realizing the loophole they snuck through. "I didn't tell them to leave me alone."

"Hey there, Wades!" Miles declares when I answer the call. "How's the honeymoon? If you wore out Clay or decided you need an annulment, you know where to find me."

"They'll find you in a locker if you don't watch it," Clay responds evenly.

I laugh. "Seriously, thank you, guys."

"What is it? What made you call so urgently?"

Sounds in the background have Miles looking away, hollering to another person.

Jay appears over his shoulder. "It's nothing. All good. It'll be here when you get back tomorrow." With a wave, Jay hangs up.

"Don't you want to deal with it?" I ask.

Clay lowers my hand holding the phone. "Nope."

"You're not worried about this season?"

"With you next to me, I'm ready for a hundred."

Thank you for reading *Game Day*! Clay and Nova have etched a place in my heart, and I hope you loved this wedding novella as much as I do.

If you can't get enough Kodiaks, I have good news: *Miles and Brooke's story is out now!*

Get ready for a steamy, banter-filled teammate's little sister romance you won't forget in **Hard to Fake**.

Keep reading for an exclusive excerpt.

Sign up for Piper Lawson's VIP list and you'll

instantly receive a steamy mini Clay and Nova bonus beach vacation story.

Join here > https://bookhip.com/GQWZRAQ

PSST! If you enjoyed Clay and Nova's sexy, grumpy sunshine romance, you'll LOVE what's next for the Denver Kodiaks.

Read a short excerpt of *Hard to Fake* below.

CHAPTER ONE
Brooke

Fake it till you make it. Isn't that what they say?

Because if we're not beautiful enough, smart enough, kind enough, capable enough, faceless people will judge us.

We try to be better.

It's easier to pretend.

"More beautiful. More natural. Just... *more, dammit.*" The photographer moves across the wooden planks, his narrowed eyes focused on the camera screen.

I push up the sleeves of my cashmere sweater and follow him.

"This isn't working," Giovanni mutters. A white man with a narrow face, it's impossible to tell if he's forty or sixty.

"What about like this?" One of the models, Aliya, tilts her head an inch in a pose that's virtually identical to her last one.

We're shooting at the Denver Botanic Gardens. The lily pond is set with stones like gems studding the cold water. In October, many of the blooms have finished for the season, but the green vegetation pops even more against the gray sky.

The models pose at the water's edge, the photographer catching reflections as they sway like flowers in the fall breeze.

Beautiful people in beautiful places doing beautiful things.

"No." Giovanni exhales. "It's the lighting." He gestures to the sun as if he can manipulate it with his hand alone.

We've been trying to make progress for hours, with nothing but dissatisfaction from the photographer. This shoot is for a national magazine, and he's going to be in trouble if he can't produce a killer result.

My eyes latch onto the male model at the front of the group—Chad, or Brad, or Thad. It's been so long since the intros we did this morning, I honestly can't remember.

He's pretty. Harmless.

Boring.

This shoot is going to waste time and money and fall flat if it doesn't have a hook.

The thought sparks something in my brain.

"Movement," I say under my breath.

"What?" Aliya demands. A high-fashion model whose star is on the rise, she has the impatience of someone who's always been told exactly how beautiful she is and thinks she can coast on her razor-sharp cheekbones and flawless skin.

"This place is too peaceful," I say. "Move *bigger*."

I pass my light reflector to another assistant and adjust my shoes. Then I step out in front of the camera onto the first of the rocks.

"Hey! Get back from..." Giovanni trails off.

I tune him out and go farther.

One of my gloves slips out of my pocket, hitting the water's surface. I bend to retrieve it, wobbling as I stick it in my pocket.

I swoop one hand up in the air at a bold angle. Then straddle two stones.

I can't paint the perfect picture, but I trust my body, my movement.

The photographer watches.

Then starts to click.

The models are giving me curious and affronted looks, as if it's better to sit around not getting the shots the client needs rather than try something new.

"Aliya, can you do that?" the photographer asks, intrigued.

I hear something that sounds like a snort. "You want me to hop on stones like a cracked out rabbit?"

"What's your name?" Giovanni asks, staring straight at me.

"Brooke."

Aliya's cold look can't kill my buzz.

I'm triumphant, basking in my moment of satisfaction. This shoot is saved, the client will be happy, and we can all move on with our lives.

A shrill screech goes up from one of the set assistants stationed near the entrance.

It's a closed set, but a man just entered and is striding over as if he owns it, his height and broad shoulders saying he's used to getting exactly what he wants.

He's big enough to block out part of the sky and attractive enough no one would mind.

The models get in on the excitement, anticipation sweeping the set like wildfire.

"Is that...?"

"No."

"Oh my God, he's so gorgeous in person."

"And tall. Damn."

Security watches him but with envious smiles rather than suspicion.

What the hell is he doing here?

My weight shifts too far to the right.

Damn it.

I tighten my abs on the opposite side trying to regain my balance.

My foot swipes for the stone but misses.

My arms windmill.

My toe tips into the icy water.

When I dressed for today in my Prada cashmere sweater and pencil skirt and suede

Stuart Weitzman ankle booties, I wasn't expecting to pull a Michael Phelps.

Swimming is not in my zone of genius. I look my best dry.

But no matter what prayers I send up to the fashion gods, the water rushes up at me like wall.

The pond is knee deep, but that's hardly a consolation when I land ass first.

It's shockingly cold, soaking through my tights and bra. I try to swallow my screech but not fast enough.

At the edge of the pond, the models are pointing and gasping.

This time it's at me.

The heat of embarrassment clashes with the numbing cold of the pond.

I wouldn't have fallen in if *someone* hadn't shown up and pulled focus from the entire editorial shoot.

The water ripples in front of me, and a hand appears. I grab it, desperate, and pull myself upright, spitting out a piece of lily pad that got plastered to my mouth.

The hand is attached to a man. One who towers over me now that I'm standing, his athlete's body hard and powerful in jeans and a bomber jacket.

Topping it all off is the most regrettably attractive face I've ever seen. Medium-brown hair with thick brows. A square, smooth-shaven jaw. A wide mouth tipped up at one corner. Eyes that have no business being so goddamned blue.

Excited murmurs go up from the models and crew. Every person here knows he's world champion Denver Kodiaks shooting guard Miles Garrett. The sexiest man in sports, possibly the world.

Women want him. Guys want to be him.

Sure, he's objectively bangable, with a killer grin, huge hands, and a body that makes you want things you can't say in front of your grandmother.

But he's also Jayden Ellis's righthand man, an extension of the basketball world I've been trying to escape from for years.

"C'mon." His voice is low and amused as he turns, motioning toward his broad back.

He must be joking.

"I'm not riding you like a horse," I scoff, picking a leaf out of my hair.

He grins, the smile of a person who enjoys it and knows he looks good doing it.

I crouch and feel for the bottom of the pond, biting my lip to hold in a whimper as the soggy, frozen cashmere plasters itself to my body.

"What are you doing?" Water soaks up to the knees of his faded-wash jeans.

"I need to find my phone." It was in my skirt pocket, and now it's not.

I bite my lip, swallowing the panic that wells up.

My life is on that. My work. My world.

The water is dark and opaque, and my foot slips. I keep searching.

On the shore, Giovanni paces. Aliya folds her arms, tapping a toe impatiently.

I take another step, feeling the bottom, and slip on something on the liner of the pool.

"Hurry up. I need to finish this shoot!" the photographer calls.

My would-be rescuer grabs me to keep me from falling. "We stay here any longer, we're going to turn into frogs."

"Only princes turn into frogs, so looks like we're both safe."

My teeth clack together from a sudden shiver that rips through me as the cold water settles into my flesh, my bones.

"Brooke Tamara Ellis." He's suddenly serious. "Your brother's going to kill me if I watch you freeze to death. Get the fuck out of this pond."

I blink at his commanding tone, my chin lifting. "Or else what?"

Before I can respond, he's hoisting me up over his shoulder in a fireman's hold.

He grabs my legs, locking them against his chest as he straightens to carry me back to shore.

My fingers dig into the muscles of his back.

It's easy to forget how freaking huge he is. Six-four and all of it muscled.

Most of the men I grew up with and went to school with liked to control women with their family name or their trust fund.

This guy literally picked me up and is carrying me through the water as if I weigh nothing.

I don't know what kind of *Princess Bride* shit this is, but I was not prepared. There's a heat starting somewhere deep in my stomach.

Stupid pro athlete.

"Miles!" Aliya rushes up to him when he sets me down on the shore on my feet, her dark hair swinging in a shiny curtain. "I can't believe you did that. What a hero!"

"Do you have a sweater? A blanket?" he asks her, his attention still on me.

"I'm fine," I protest.

"Brock says she's fine, Miles."

"It's Brooke," I start, but I'm distracted by his hands on my upper arms.

"We're almost done here, then I'll be ready to go..." Aliya continues as if I hadn't spoken. There's impatience now and a distracted smile.

I look between them and realize the truth.

He's here for her.

Because he's a massive basketball star and she's a model.

Beautiful people doing beautiful people things.

"It was her own fault," Aliya continues. "She was supposed to be a shoot assistant."

The embarrassment dials up to humiliation.

On my own social media, I'm in front of a camera, contributing to the fantasy life of being a twenty-something without a care in the world except for curating an enviable designer shoe collection and snapping pics of the latest appetizer at a hot new restaurant with my friends.

Today, I was carrying cameras and checking lighting.

My teeth chatter again. "I need to get back to work." I pull out of Miles's grasp and look around for some equipment that needs wrangling.

"You're fired," Giovanni declares. "I cannot have assistants disrupting my shoot."

I wring out the bottom of my sweater, water hitting the deck with a stream of plinks. Indignation edges into my despair.

"Aliya, I need to drive Brooke home," Miles says before I can respond.

"You what?!" We blurt it at the same time.

Aliya's penciled brows drag together as though she's calculating whether she could shove me back in the water and drown me.

I trail him to the parking lot.

"I have a car," I call after him.

"I'll have it dropped off later. Give me your keys."

"No way."

Miles hits the locks and opens the passenger door. "You can drip all over your leather or all over mine."

He's tall enough to easily rest an elbow along the top. His other hand opens, waiting.

I turn it over.

Getting my car detailed was not in my plans for the week.

I drop my keys into his open palm and get in the passenger side.

"You wanted to swim, you could've done it in July rather than the end of October," he suggests as he shifts into the driver's seat.

I pry a piece of curling hair off my forehead. "I had a plan."

"A wet plan?"

So much for the straightening job that took me an hour.

I'm tempted to toss my hair out of pettiness and watch the droplets spatter his interior, but it would be a crime against the beautiful leather.

"It was going perfectly until you showed up," I inform him.

He snorts and reaches for the vents in front of me, angling them so warm air blows at me.

"Why were you working behind the camera?" he asks.

"Thought I'd broaden my horizons. Learn more about the other side of the industry." I shift in my seat. "What's up with you and Aliya? I didn't know you were dating."

"Wouldn't go that far."

"Ahh, the truth comes out. So, she DM'd you a pic of her topless and you agreed to dinner."

"Or I sent her a pic of me bottomless." He winks and starts to whistle along with the radio.

Miles is the chillest guy I've ever met. Everyone loves him: his teammates, his competition, and every female basketball fan in the country.

But he's not larger than life to me like he is to the rest of the basketball world.

So what if once in a while when his grin lasts too long, it makes my stomach flip?

It's a natural reaction to a hot-AF man. Nothing personal.

"You're not whistling to Kendrick right now," I say.

"The ladies love it."

When he hits the chorus, I can't stop the eye roll.

The heating system starts to send warm air in earnest, and it feels good. I groan and stretch my fingers toward the heat.

Without looking over, Miles turns it up more.

At a light, he reaches into the back seat and retrieves a sweatshirt, dropping it in my lap.

"What size is this, Sasquatch?" I hoist an arm of the giant cotton form into the air.

"I'll find you something else to wear if you tell me why you were really working on that shoot."

My mouth falls open.

Miles's popsicle-chill vibe can lull you into thinking he's safe, but when he cares about something, he'll dig in with a stubbornness even my mom would admire.

Being the only daughter of a United States senator sounds like a good deal, especially for someone who enjoys being in the spotlight. What you don't realize is that it comes with strings. A lot of them.

Especially in our family.

Be intelligent, but not edgy.

Be polite, but not a pushover.

Be presentable, but conservatively so.

Which, according to my mother, was the cause of her voicemail last week that changed everything.

It's my dirty secret, and I'm not about to share it with anyone, least of all my brother's gorgeous, rich, popular teammate.

I'm already embarrassed, but confessing why I was there would dial that up to off-the-charts humiliation.

"Don't look," I say. I'm not usually self-conscious, but this day has thrown me for a loop.

"Wouldn't dream of it."

With a glance toward Miles to ensure he's watching the road, I peel off the sweater. The warm air feels like heaven on my bare skin as I tug the sweatshirt over my head. It smells clean and a little like Miles. Once I've tugged it down, leaving a pool of fabric around my body, I reach inside to work off my bra.

Who invented these things? I'm half an inch from to dislocating my shoulder.

A few grunts later, I drop the bra in a soggy pile in my lap.

"You want a medal for that performance?" Miles drawls, navigating traffic.

"It's the least you can do," I retort.

It's not though.

He dragged me out of the pond, got himself soaked in the process, and blew off his date to drive me home.

Miles is one of the good guys.

I shove the shirt sleeves up my arms, feeling like the Michelin man from all the wrinkles.

Miles's gaze flicks over and lands on the stack, my teal lace bra on top. "Lace, huh?"

"Stop it."

He grins, but his attention stays where it is.

"Um. Miles, the light—"

"Shit." He hits the brakes as the yellow switches to red.

I'm tossed forward, the seatbelt lock engaging with a snap across my shoulders.

The last few blocks of the drive pass in silence. Miles pulls up in front of my building without asking for the address.

"Need me to come up to wring your hair out and tuck you in?"

"No, thank you. You're not the only one with a date tonight," I announce.

I get the briefest satisfaction of seeing his eyes narrow in a very un-Miles way before I get out of the car and slam the door.

End of Sample
To continue reading, pick up _Hard to Fake_ at your favorite retailer.

DENVER KODIAKS SERIES

It's not every day you ask your older brother's teammate to be your fake boyfriend. But desperate times call for gorgeous, impulsive measures.

Denver Kodiaks is a steamy, brother's teammate sports romance about a sorority reunion, a college crush, and a love that's bigger than basketball.

KING OF THE COURT SERIES

After being dumped and losing my job the same week, the last thing my broken heart needs is a rebound.

A steamy, grumpy sunshine sports romance featuring a woman down on her luck, a star basketball player with a filthy mouth, and a connection neither of them can deny.

OFF-LIMITS SERIES

Turns out the beautiful man from the club is my new professor… But he wasn't when he kissed me.

Off-Limits is a forbidden age gap college romance series. Find out what happens when the beautiful man from the club is Olivia's hot new professor.

WICKED SERIES

Rockstars don't chase college students. But Jax Jamieson never followed the rules.

Wicked is a new adult rock star series full of nerdy girls, hot rock stars, pet skunks, and ensemble casts you'll want to be friends with forever.

RIVALS SERIES

At seventeen, I offered Tyler Adams my home, my life, my heart. He stole them all.

Rivals is an angsty new adult series. Fans of forbidden romance, enemies to lovers, friends to lovers, and rock star romance will love these books.

ENEMIES SERIES

I sold my soul to a man I hate. Now, he owns me.

Enemies is an enthralling, explosive romance about an American DJ and a British billionaire. If you like wealthy, royal alpha males, enemies to lovers, travel or sexy romance, this series is for you!

TRAVESTY SERIES

My best friend's brother grew up. Hot.

Travesty is a steamy romance series following best friends who start a fashion label from NYC to LA. It contains best friends brother, second chances, enemies to lovers, opposites attract and friends to lovers stories. If you like sexy, sassy romances, you'll love this series.

PLAY SERIES

I know what I want. It's not Max Donovan. To hell with his money, his gaming empire, and his joystick.

Play is an addictive series of standalone romances with slow burn tension, delicious banter, office romance and unforgettable characters. If you like smart, quirky, steamy enemies-to-lovers, contemporary romance, you'll love Play.

MODERN ROMANCE SERIES

When your rich, handsome best friend asks you to be his fake girlfriend? Say no.

Modern Romance is a smart, sexy series of contemporary romances following a set of female friends running a relationship marketing company in NYC. If you enjoy hot guys who treat their families like gold, fun antics, dirty talk, real characters, steamy scenes, badass heroines and smart banter, you'll love the Modern Romance series.

ABOUT THE AUTHOR

Piper Lawson is a *WSJ* and *USA Today* bestselling author of smart and steamy romance.

She writes women who follow their dreams, best friends who know your dirty secrets and love you anyway, and complex heroes you'll fall hard for.

Piper lives in Canada with her tall and brilliant husband. She's a sucker for dark eyes, dark coffee, and dark chocolate.

For a complete reading list, visit
www.piperlawsonbooks.com/books

**Subscribe to Piper's VIP email list
www.piperlawsonbooks.com/
subscribe**

amazon.com/author/piperlawson

bookbub.com/authors/piper-lawson

instagram.com/piperlawsonbooks

tiktok.com/@piperlawsonbooks

facebook.com/piperlawsonbooks

goodreads.com/piperlawson

ACKNOWLEDGMENTS

Thank you for reading *Game Day*! You know I love a wedding story almost as much as the highs and lows of fighting for an HEA. With luck, this little slice of Kodiak cake gave you all the feels and closure, and got you hyped for *Hard to Fake*.

This story wouldn't have happened without the support of my awesome readers, including my ARC readers! You ladies provide endless enthusiasm, cheerleading, early feedback, and help spreading the word. I am endlessly grateful.

Cassie Robertson: Thank you for bringing consistency to my wacky ideas, and for laughing at my jokes in the margins (but only the good ones).

Devon Burke: Thank you for helping polish my stories into their best selves, and for bringing your incredible heart and wisdom to the task.

Annette Brignac and Kate Tilton: Thank you for being in my corner, for seeing what I'm trying to create in the world and creating it with me. Without you, few things would get done and probably none of it would get done well.

Lori Jackson and Emily Wittig: Thank you for taking my random ideas and wacky gradients and making art from them. I'm grateful you still respond to my emails.

Nina Grinstead and the entire VPR team: thank you for your wisdom, support, and tireless effort to help readers find books they'll love.

Last but not least, thank YOU for reading. Truly. Knowing we're living in these words and worlds together is the best part of any gig I've ever had.

Love always,
Piper